Knee-Deep in Cinders

Ashley Capes

Chapter 1.

Vilas tossed his book onto a polished table at the sound of footfalls beyond his gilded cage – odd, since feeding time was not for at least an hour. *Another Radiant come to prod at me?*

He rose with a frown, starting for the chamber door. On his way, he ducked between the wilder of his hanging plants to pause within a golden glow. Cast by the admittedly generous skylight above, it still didn't change the fact that he was a prisoner. A sweet scent lingered as he glared at the entryway and its door.

At the pile of splinters and ash it could have been.

Should have been.

After all, it was just a pathetically normal door. Oak, with a single steel bolt. One blow ought to have shattered the thing, sent smouldering wreckage into the corridor beyond. Yet he had not managed even a single scratch in years.

He tapped two fingers upon the silver collar at his neck as he lifted his voice. "I am not interested in whatever you have to say, whoever you are."

Fracture-thin lines of yellow gleamed within the wood-grain as the magic seal lifted. The door swung open to reveal a pair of Radiants in their white vests and cloaks, hands dripping with silver rings.

Neither spoke, merely watched him.

"Yes?" At least their clothing bore no tint of azure. *Never a good start to the visit.* Vilas folded his arms. "I am still sealed away, as you are aware. Have you really come to interrupt my reading by simply standing in silence?"

Still no response.

Usually, unexpected visits came with Radiant Healers and their sticky minds... Or at least, the same old questions about the war and his own abilities. Sometimes, those questions were followed by petty lords and ladies desperate to catch a glimpse of 'Vilas, the Beast of Khiya'.

And each time, the collar disappointed them.

Only good thing about it.

But today, his visitor was no idle nobleman trying to impress a lover, or a gaggle of youths fulfilling a dare. No.

Today was suddenly a little brighter.

Queen Ima herself strode into his prison, preceded by two more Radiants, each man bearing tattoos of torches on their cheeks, a symbol of additional power, something common among the Luminaries themselves. *Excessive.*

She didn't need either pair of guards.

The Onathian Queen wore her dark hair shorter than other ladies of the court, painted shadows shaped as pears around her eyes – a trend which had, apparently, caught on in the rest of the palace and city itself.

Quite a change from the Onath of old.

Even her eyelids had been shaded in a soft red.

And when she smiled at him, it was the smile that quickened his pulse, that tormented his dreams.

But he did not welcome her.

She approached, near enough to touch. Perfume of vanilla and orange blossom almost drew him closer still, but he did not lean in. Her crimson gown hugged her hips and breasts, the lace at its edges patterned as flowers, though in contrast, the black gloves on her bare arms were not made to flatter... but to protect.

Deadly, indeed.

Something that only made her all the more alluring. *Just how much would it hurt if her hands touched me?* Despite his reading, even after years of research, the source of her strange power was a mystery... useful though it could prove to be.

"Vilas." She glanced around his chambers; chair, table, bed half-visible in the adjoining room. "You still seem comfortable enough, despite claims in your recent... correspondence."

Highly unlikely that any of his churlish letters about minor inconveniences and otherwise had prompted her visit. "Your Majesty."

Queen Ima sat on his chair and sifted through the books he had collected. Just what was her game? She was not interested in his reading material. After all, her puppets approved – or rejected – everything he requested. Ima knew exactly what he was reading. She wanted something.

"I'm studying the Western Rebellion," he said. *Among other things in that language.* "I don't believe I have time to read to you."

She opened one of the books and closed it after a moment. "I can read the Western language, as you are aware, handsome."

"Yet I cannot fathom this visit, Your Majesty."

She crossed her legs and leant back, hints of her calf visible, drawing his eye though he ought not to have let himself be distracted. "Have you heard of the Cherished Sons?"

"If you mean that insipid cult from the Wastelands, then a little. Why?"

"I do mean them, yes."

"Frankly, they do not seem worth your attention."

"Yet, I would hear more of your opinion."

He shrugged. "I'm surprised they've persisted so long. I heard them speaking once, Your Majesty. If he had opened his mouth and mulch poured forth, it would have been more coherent. What possible concern could they be for the Queen of Onath?"

"The Cherished Sons have changed, and I believe,

are not to be underestimated."

"Oh?"

She leant forward and her perfume became more distinct – definitely vanilla and orange blossoms – but her eyes were more compelling, dark and glittering with determination. "No longer are they so few. Their numbers have grown, and lately, swiftly. They are drawing the young and bitter from outlying villages, and even the city itself now. We intercepted two weapon-shipments in the spring alone. They have funds and they are preparing."

"For what?" It was a noteworthy change from the cult's past activities of lonely sermons and graffiti in the city, or rituals in the Wastelands but certainly nothing that couldn't be countered quite easily by the Radiants. Or Gosdan and the army. After all, Onath boasted one of the largest forces in all the nations. "The return of their Twin Prophets, was it?"

She replaced his book with a sigh. "I've no doubt that's exactly what is being sold to the vulnerable and the foolish. But whoever is behind this development has a very real target – Otakom Dam."

"That would be more troubling," he replied, but after a moment, spread his hands. "Nevertheless, it must be far worse than what you've mentioned so far, if you've been given permission to seek out one such as I."

Ima raised an eyebrow, though she still smiled. "Permission? Don't bother trying to insult me, Vilas.

Just listen. I need the Beast of Khiya."

"Why? And what are you offering? Freedom?" He gestured to the collar, and it was impossible to keep a sudden anger from his voice. "Because I haven't given up on my oath. I will destroy this city if you free me. It is the very least I can do."

She narrowed her eyes. "Even the innocents?"

He slammed a fist onto the table. "Don't even *think* about lecturing me, Your Majesty."

A chill shot through his collar as it constricted. Air vanished. Edges dug deep into his skin and Vilas collapsed to the carpet, clawing at his throat.

The room grew dim.

"Enough." The queen's voice rang out.

Vilas sucked in air from where he lay upon the carpet. Slowly, his vision cleared as the collar loosened, growing warmer as it did.

Queen Ima knelt on one knee beside his head – pinning his hair. Vilas heard a gasp from one of the Radiants but she waved off the man's protest. "This isn't the time for propriety, Hosun."

"But... Your Majesty, the Royal Person need never stoop, even for so much as a gold stalk, let alone this murderous beast. We do not need him. We should send another infiltrator instead." His eyes were wide. "You must let –"

"I must?" Her voice no longer held any trace of patience.

The Radiant placed both hands behind his back and

receded. "Forgive me."

Ima did not respond. Instead, she pointed a gloved finger at Vilas. "You can paint me with my grandfather's mistakes from decades long gone all you wish, but I will have an answer. Once more, I need the Beast of Khiya and *you* want freedom. Help me wipe out the Cherished Sons."

The black velvet of the glove was close. All she had to do was remove it and brush against him and the pain... He sighed up at the queen. "And again, I ask. Why me?"

"For all the reasons I have given."

He frowned. "And?"

"And because we found traces of Brutes. Or at least, a Brute." She lifted her knee. "And so it must be you, Vilas."

He met her unflinching gaze.

Brutes. Called giant, ogre or sometimes simply monsters. Not a single name was inaccurate *precisely*, but the Wahkyog were more intelligent, more human than such descriptions suggested. Fled, vanished, vanquished, extinct... supposedly. None knew the truth, but it had been *many* years since they were last seen.

Even by my standards.

The Brutes were no friend of his own ancestors either, but why had they returned now? To Onath? Assuming any of the queen's claims were true. *Above all, why would the Wahkyog work with a bottom-feeding cult? It is not their way either.*

Whatever the truth, it was an enormous request. "I might be able to stop them – without my bonds, of course."

"Name your price."

Chapter 2.

The queen stepped aside.

Vilas pushed his hair back as he rose. He returned to the table and settled into his chair with a sigh. Ima watched him without comment, and he did not answer at first. But it was not a ploy. No such pantomime was necessary – the answer he would give was obvious to all. The Brutes were worthy of more consideration, considering their size, strength, and the enormous barrier of communication between them. How to negotiate with a cold mountain, after all?

Was the Beast of Khiya an actual match for the Wahkyog?

For even *one*?

Vilas rubbed the stubble on his cheek. The freedom he would demand, would it end up being nothing more than the freedom to die at the hands of an old enemy? Leaving vengeance against the city unfulfilled? *What a Godsforsaken waste that would be.*

Above all, Queen Ima had little incentive to keep her word, given his promise to destroy Onath and its sparkling streets.

Ima folded her arms. "Is it such a difficult decision?"

"Not at all." He rose to stand before her. "I do, of course, demand my freedom for this service."

"Once you have dealt with the Brutes," she answered with a nod.

"And you," he said.

She paused. "And what?"

"I will save this cursed city from the Wahkyog if I can share your bed, Your Majesty."

Cries of outrage burst from the Radiants, and one younger man trembled where he stood, nostrils widening.

Ima raised a hand, a slight smile upon her lips. "So small a price, Vilas?"

"I would not underestimate you that way."

She removed one glove and reached out to touch his cheek, the barest grazing, and a thrill cascaded across his skin, like standing ever-so close to a bolt of lightning. "If you succeed – and survive – we have a deal."

Radiant Hosun stepped forward, his fellows right behind the man. "I must object, My Queen!"

"You think a single night is too much to give to save my people, Radiant?" She replaced her glove. "Please grow up. This is life and death for *tens of thousands* of people. More."

The man flushed but did not step down, even waving his ringed hands. "But there is no guarantee. How do we know that he will keep his word? That he'll even be *able* to succeed, Your Majesty? And even if he does, all know about his sworn vengeance."

"We're here because there is no-one else. It is that simple." She turned back to Vilas. "There are further conditions on your freedom."

"Minders."

She nodded. "Hosun here is sending along his strongest; a young man named Tano, as part of a group that includes soldiers and a Steel Maiden. The party will be led by Gosdan Machical, whose orders you will follow. You are leaving for the walls immediately. Do you still accept?"

"I do." He managed not to grind the words out. The possible return of the Brutes was one thing, but Machical? That filth? The mutt who cut the silken ropes of Khiya – and worse. *This will be... difficult.* Knowing the general was still alive but never seeing him was not at all the same as knowing the man lived and having to meet face-to-face.

"Young Tano will be along with your escort soon." Queen Ima smiled from the doorway, then left the room, a pair of servants trailing.

The remaining Radiants too, moved to follow their queen but before the door was sealed again, Hosun stopped in the arch. "I will kill you myself, should you lay a finger upon her."

Vilas shrugged. "Threatening me makes me wonder if I should leave this room at all."

"Ha. You want your freedom."

"In its place, I do enjoy time to read. Lovely meals, even for Onathian-fare, a comfortable bed – beautiful flowers too. Time to sit and plot and plan."

Hosun sneered. "She's not going to sleep with you. Surely you know that. She's betting on you defeating the Brutes and dying in the process. That, or she'll simply keep you trapped, once you've served your purpose."

"Only time will tell," Vilas said with a grin.

But once Hosun had spun on his heel to storm out, slamming and then Binding the door behind him, Vilas grunted. The weasel might not have been too far wrong. Sharing Ima's bed was one thing, but she would not simply let him destroy Onath.

Even so, she is the key.

And his vengeance would not be abandoned.

Life had suddenly become interesting. Or at the very least, no longer a mind-numbing routine of sameness with slight variations from week to week. He chuckled at the surge of vitality that followed. "Is this fresh hope, then?" *Fascinating.* Something that had been missing for the last... how many years?

Vilas stacked his books into a neat pile, taking care with the one detailing the unfathomable power of Ima's lineage, then strode to the bedroom. There, he opened the ornate dresser and withdrew his Maelohas tunic from amongst the Onath blues and whites. Black, save for the striped silver thread on the sleeves, it still bore traces of old blood.

And a hole from Machical's blade.

An echo of pain ran through Vilas' side but he ignored it, instead lifting the sleeve to examine the silver. Faded but not wholly dulled, the patterns still appeared as a pair of linked hands.

For the first... dozen years of captivity, he'd worn the tunic each day.

Petty defiance, nothing more. Yet in time, the very sight of the fabric had him avoiding mirrors and eventually, the black was hidden away. In the many years that followed, it remained therein.

But the soft hemp could be worn again, even if doing so would drag a stinging bitterness back into the light.

No other piece of clothing like it in the world now.

Vilas removed his plain robe, running a hand across the still-raised scar on the skin at his side, a scar which would line up precisely with the hole in his tunic. But he placed the last shred of his people, of Maelohas, on with a sigh. *Strange to come home now... even in this tiny way.*

Next, the chest at the bottom.

Hinges on the lid squeaked as he lifted the top.

Inside, two items only. A thin blade of steel that bore faint blue for its handle, and a feathered quill. The quill sat empty of ink, save for the old stains. Its feather was a dark grey, with a golden triangle pattern, which in turn bore smaller, pale triangles within.

On the lyrebird, it made for quite a magnificent display.

"Yet another thing long-since gone now, I imagine." Vilas lifted the quill free but did not take it. *That life is gone.*

Instead, he took the knife.

Next, he strode to the opposite wall, kneeling on his half-made bed – two paintings, each of Maelohas. Of a Maelohas that no longer existed. The city of Khiya, stones aglow at sunset and the sweet Sighing Forest, as seen from the mountain peaks.

All gone now; destroyed by King Hevolma's greed.

Over the years, a few Radiants had remarked upon the paintings – either in surprise that he had made them, or to ask why he kept such depressing things. Such painful things, memories of things that had been destroyed by 'war', as they claimed. Sometimes, it took considerable effort not to try throttling the fools – all the more galling was their ignorance, that they dared use the word 'depressing'.

Or 'war'.

A bare-faced lie.

The obvious answer Vilas might have given, had even a single Radiant been worthy of it, was that the reminder of such places fed his fury. Kept it full and leering, claws ever-sharp as they ground against the pain.

Of course, even his lack of answer would always be noted in their journals.

And what had they learnt? Nothing, it seemed. Not even from the blood, hair, and nails they used to take, back in the early days.

Never stops them from asking the same old questions.

Vilas returned to the entryway. There, he leant against the wall to wait, glancing around the room. The table caught his eye, a place where he read and read and read all manner of book, scroll and scrap. That and its chair. The third he'd been given after the first two were broken.

One in rage, and the second in an accident when watering the hanging plants.

Am I suddenly cataloguing things for memory? I will not miss this place. Not even the plants and their sweet little flowers of yellow.

Finally, the faint vibration of *their* approach came, a bare tingle against his collar.

"Bah." Would Gosdan Machical himself be along with the escort, walking through the palace and out into the streets? Or would the general instead choose to wait in the city? At the enormous Eastern Gate, with their inlay of twisted minerals, perhaps.

A twinge in his side.

"And just how have the years treated you, Butcher?" Vilas murmured.

But when thin lines of searing yellow appeared then faded, seal lifted, and the door opened, three

Radiants stood outside but no Gosdan Machical. Vilas unclenched a fist. *When exactly did I make that?*

Two of the men were older, their white clothing immaculate, expressions decidedly unwelcoming. One moved with a familiar glint to the eye, something that suggested he was eager for a chance to use the collar.

It was, sadly, all too easy enough for any Radiant to activate the constriction.

The third was their leader, obviously the young fellow Ima mentioned by name, Tano.

Not a child by any stretch, yet nor had he been a man for many years. His blond hair was tied into a plait, and he wore a thin beard and moustache. His bearing was quite calm as he examined Vilas. Quite different from their customary expressions; predatory curiosity or barely contained disgust.

Nor had he reached the standing of Luminary, considering the lack of tattoos on his cheeks. And still, he was the strongest, according to the queen.

"First time seeing the last of the Maelohas?" Vilas asked.

Tano inclined his head in a slight acknowledgement. "Her Majesty expects us to join Gosdan Machical immediately. Are you ready to leave?"

"I am," Vilas replied. A somewhat more polite Radiant, it seemed. "Obviously, I have no provisions."

"All has been arranged. Follow me."

The Radiant led him down the darkened hall of stone, his fellows falling into step at the rear. Vilas could have smiled. *I'm not planning on fleeing, you fools.*

Even if he did, the collar would ensure he did not get far.

Little had changed in the year since he'd last left his rooms – nor from the five years before it, in turn. The halls were still polished black marble threaded with white veins. No windows here. Instead, standing lamps had been forged to resemble longswords, giving off a simmering, magical light that lacked the warmth of fire.

But his escort did not stay in such gleaming corridors for long, soon turning down a narrow set of stairs that ended in a dark storeroom – or what would have been one, had it contained anything. Instead, just a faint sheen of dampness to the bluestone, a faint glow from the Radiants themselves now their only light source.

"I'm surprised I'm not being paraded."

Tano approached the far wall and stretched his arms to press upon a pair of stones. "Are you?"

Stone rumbled as a piece of the wall slid aside, revealing more shadow.

"It's a missed opportunity for Ima. She could have demonstrated her power, cowed her rivals."

"Do you believe she has that need?" Tano asked as he waved them into the passage.

"I do not know their names, but they exist. All strong leaders face their share of jealousy and resentment. I imagine her grandfather and his lackeys, for one."

"Perhaps a few holdovers from His Majesty's reign, yes," he said with a shrug.

"And they don't worry you?"

Tano almost seemed to smile in the dim glow of his power. "You've met Ima more than enough to know the answer to that."

He chuckled. "So I have."

From behind, one of the Radiants muttered.

"Is something amiss, Mardoa?" Tano asked.

A moment of hesitation. "No. I just don't believe we should be treating him like a companion."

"Is that what you think is happening here?" Tano had not stopped. "He will help us save the city, and for that, he receives my courtesy while we travel together. I have not befriended a war-criminal simply because I have manners."

"Well..."

The conversation trailed off. Vilas smiled. Interesting lad. *And does he understand that the feeling is no doubt mutual?*

The passage descended four more sets of stairs before the soft rush of flowing water grew audible; an underground river in a small cavern. From either end, darkness waited, interrupted by old, whale-shaped lamps. Their light offered little detail, but it was noteworthy insomuch as the city of Onath had been landlocked for five centuries.

Making the body of water of interest.

An unattended longboat waited at a shadowy dock.

Tano led them aboard, letting the other Radiants pole them into the cold current. Vilas leant back, staring at nothing in particular as the boat picked up speed. His young jailor did not appear battle-hardened but then, appearances were almost never conclusive. Noble-born, considering his status as a Radiant, he would at least be highly-educated. Whether he'd be useful against the Brutes... he was, supposedly, the strongest.

After a time, the young man turned to Vilas. "Have you faced the Wahkyog before?"

"How old do I look, exactly?"

Tano shrugged. "A grown man. The silver in your hair conflicts with an only moderate amount of lines upon your face, but all know that the Maelohas lived longer than the rest of us."

"We did. But I have not faced the Brutes." *Father and mother might have.*

"A shame."

Vilas leant forward. "The queen shared few details about the traces found. Have you seen the evidence yourself?"

"Yes. Gosdan Machical has custody of the corpse."

"A corpse? That's more than a trace. Tell me."

The Radiant shook his head. "Trace might still be accurate. It was only a few pieces. Most of the body had been eaten by scavengers. Those, too, we found dead amongst the blood. The Brute had fallen from the dam wall, you see."

"The blood is poisonous to most animals, but they are drawn to it."

"Well, what they had failed to ingest was part of a torso and half a hand. It was not only the granite-texture of the deep-blue skin, but the sheer size of the heart. Or what was left of it – no man could have borne such a thing in his chest."

"What of the hand and torso?" Vilas asked. "Did either bear the markings like ink? In orange?"

Tano nodded. "Some were visible. There is no doubt in my mind that what we found matches the creatures described in the old songs and legends."

"Then the question becomes whether this was a single Brute, the last one, lost and wandering, having simply fallen? And whether there truly is a link between the body and the Cherished Sons."

"We believe it so."

Vilas nodded. "So I have heard. Why?"

"For one, it is because the cultists have taken to painting themselves in similar patterns of blue and orange. Their work matches far more closely the body than what history books appeared to have distorted or forgotten."

"Hmmm." Evidence *did* seem to be mounting. On the other hand, the cult members could just as easily copied designs found on the Brute's corpse, and were still planning to attack the dam themselves. The Wahkyog didn't need to have made a return for that to be true.

And yet, what if... "We'll be examining the remains first, then?"

"Gosdan Machical will decide that," Tano replied, then paused. "Will that be a problem for you?"

"That depends on His Radiance."

"The general is more than able to set aside your differences for the good of the city."

"That's a very diplomatic word there."

"Which word?"

"Differences."

Tano narrowed his eyes. "How so?"

Vilas leant back against the gunwale. *Have I found a nerve already, then?* "I'll let you do your own reading."

"I am extremely well-read when it comes to the Maelohas-incursion."

"And of the two of us, I was the only one present at your 'incursion', lad."

Tano stiffened, but his response was cut off by an announcement from one of the other Radiants. "Approaching the dock."

Chapter 3.

After climbing onto the darkened dock and ascending another cold stairway, Vilas found himself struggling to keep a lid on a new disgust. On his fury too, but he did not lash out. He *did* stop walking, however. "Do you have nothing else to use?"

So far, in the absence of torches or lamps, they had travelled by light of so-called glow-bones carried by his jailors.

"What?" One of the Radiants frowned over his shoulder.

"A lamp. Or your own gifts – make an Obedient Light rather than that bone."

Now all three Radiants had stopped. The two older ones glanced at each other a moment before one snorted and then they climbed on.

"Give me your names," Vilas said through clenched teeth.

They continued to walk. "Why?"

"So that I can kill you once I am free," he called after.

Tano raised his voice. "Enough. Put them away for now," he told the others, his voice short. To Vilas, he spoke with equal dissatisfaction. "You are to obey, remember?"

"I have not disobeyed any order."

"It's a reminder. Keep walking."

"Remind them that my people's bones are not tools to save them time simply because they are lazy," Vilas said as he resumed his climb.

Tano did not answer.

Vilas glared up at the other two but let his anger simmer down, imagining the two Radiants exploding in an eruption of molten flame; almost enough to satisfy him for the time being.

Eventually, the climb came to an end, stopping at an iron grate. It featured only a narrow grid that was surely difficult for even a rat to find a way through. Long captivity ensured he would not be able to judge exactly what part of the city it led to, but likely somewhere beyond the palace walls. Even a famously secure place like Onath would have a few escape holes.

His last visit to the streets did little to aid his memory now.

If nothing else, I was able to upset the court. Few had enjoyed his comments at the time, but Ima's grandfather seemed insistent that he attend the Open-Air Night-Ball. *Like a trophy.*

And while it had taken King Hevolma a little too long to arrange for a gag once Vilas started denouncing those who'd gathered – the bastard had certainly been up to something new before his failing health forced him to hand the throne to his short-lived son.

One regret that would come with destroying the city was not being able to personally witness Hevolma's death.

Tano stopped.

The Radiant extended a hand before the grate and the faintest traces of rigid, yellow lines grew visible.

"Vilas. Within the city walls, and beyond, you are to follow our instructions. You are not to bring harm to even a single citizen through either action or inaction. Gosdan Machical leads but you are to obey me and any other Radiant. Any soldier we travel with too, for that matter," he explained. "Anything you suspect or discover about the Brutes you reveal immediately. Similarly for the Cherished Sons. You will take any and every action required to save the dam *and* protect the lives within the city. Understood?"

Vilas tapped the collar. "This ensures my compliance, as we both know."

"I would hear the words."

"I will obey."

Tano nodded, then lifted the seal on the grate. Yellow gridlines flared through the steel and penetrated some of the way into the stone walls too. Together, the three Radiants lifted the gate and once Vilas passed through, they sealed the way once more.

Yet another narrow passage and yet another sealed door waited beyond, this one opening into a long, climbing stairwell. Thin windows admitted enough light to see a little better.

Halfway up, perhaps at ground level, Tano unsealed a final grate and this time, revealed full daylight. It streamed in between tall walls and fell across a garden plot, greenery climbing.

From Vilas' vantage point, the streets of Onath lived in glimpses only – a flow of blue and white tunics, sometimes shades of grey, sometimes brighter colours too, all just visible through bars that ringed the entry. And only a murmur came with the movement rather than the roar of a crowd, in spite of such steady numbers.

Not reminiscent of the Onath of old.

But what caught his eye, as Tano led the way through the gate and into the cobbled street, was an old fellow wearing a black armband. The armband had been stitched with white thread; a dew drop… or a tear. The gesture was a relic of decades gone by, and something that brought the war to mind in a sharper sense than he'd expected.

The man leant against the wall, pack at his feet, watching the crowds, and when he noticed the Radiants, he narrowed his eyes.

One of Tano's seconds sneered at the old man in response, but no words were exchanged.

Interesting.

For some, those with longer memories perhaps, few fond ones existed of the war; the way the Radiants and the army seized the city's resources. And lives. Even of the locals.

Here, far from the homes of the wealthy, the murmur of voices was joined by somewhat rhythmic growls from two beasts of burden being fed on a corner, the shaggy creatures standing beneath the sign for a stable. The clatter of horse-hooves, too, reached Vilas and together it all masked whatever Tano and the other Radiants were discussing where they walked just ahead.

But now that Vilas could see farther than a few dozen paces... there, the unbreakable Eastern Gate – a patch of darkness beneath the clear sky above. Another twinge in his side, and he reached for the old wound, but it had not started to bleed; the warmth was a phantom he would never banish.

The Gates towered over the stone and wooden buildings below, doors fit for giants, each mammoth hunk of stone the size of an inn. *Nothing* could penetrate them, and the black inlay of stored magic that ran across their surface in jagged patterns was so powerful that two score Radiants were required to close and open them.

And above all, not even the Embers of the Maelohas could break through.

As well I know.

A group of figures below the gate were not close

enough to make out many details, but gleaming steel suggested Gosdan Machical waited with a squad of soldiers.

Exactly as promised by both the queen and Tano.

Even so, actually coming face-to-face with the man now, after so many years…

Vilas ground his teeth. *Gods, the blight on all life isn't even visible.* And yet, the only thing protecting the Gosdan was the collar. Tano and the other two, the homes around them, all would be a pile of smouldering ashes without the collar, Machical himself following shortly thereafter.

"I trust you are not thinking of some futile escape attempt." Tano had paused to allow a small group of children to pass, their faces half-concealed by armfuls of clothing, giggles rising.

"What else can you tell me about the pieces found at the dam?" Vilas asked, instead of answering the man's question.

Tano's reply was interrupted by the approach of a nobleman in armour and yellow cloak that almost brushed the stones. His dark beard had been shaped into twin points, yet despite the 'affectation', his smile lacked the artifice common to the nobility… a well-practiced expression, nevertheless? Tano inclined his head. "Lord Noriam."

"Radiant Tano, it is a pleasure to meet you on this rather significant day."

"I hope it so."

The nobleman spread his hands, eyes drifting to Vilas. Noriam was not one that ever came to catch a glimpse of the 'Beast of Khiya' over the years, nor was his name familiar. A distant relative of one of the lesser families? "Vilas of Maelohas. I trust you are working with the best interests of the city in your heart."

Vilas raised an eyebrow. "That is naive of you."

Lord Noriam chuckled. "Well. Perhaps it is more fitting for me to say instead, whatever deal you have struck with the queen, I hope it will actually benefit Onath."

"We appreciate your kind wishes, Lord Noriam," Tano said. "We must meet with the Gosdan, however."

The nobleman stepped aside. "Of course, of course."

They passed by and Vilas looked back at one point when the sense of the man's following gaze grew strong. And Lord Noriam was indeed watching, his calm expression revealing little – or concealing much. "I am not familiar with that one," Vilas said.

Tano shrugged. "In the court, he is said to bridge the political span between Queen Ima's eye for the future and the more… settled nobles who favour policies of her grandfather."

"I see." Such an answer may well have explained Noriam's interest – and knowledge of their path – but the gate and Machical were growing closer, and thus more pressing. *Time to stand before the true beast.*

After fifty long years.

For the first time since Machical led his genocidal

soldiers into Maelohas, joined by the Luminaries and other Radiants, and for the first time since Vilas and his few remaining companions chased the 'victorious' monsters back to their lair, since obliterating those forces at the gate, since crashing against its surface over and over, since a profound exhaustion dragged against him with every step, and since actually finding the Gosdan that day, only to meet the man's filthy blade… After *everything* it took simply to fail, his friends lost, his strength vanishing, and since catching only a final glimpse of Machical's bloody leer before collapsing…

… it stung to see the man alive and well now.

Vilas kept his back straight as he neared. His jaw was clenched so hard again, already it had begun to ache. But he controlled his limbs, controlled the futile but searing urge to unleash a column of flame upon the man.

Futile and equally pitiful, since the collar would do its foul work.

Gosdan Machical waited before his men, arms folded.

White hair now covered the man's head and his cheeks; his face was deeply lined but those cold, blue eyes had not softened. Nor had his frame, it seemed, by the ease with which he wore his armour – the breastplate polished and pauldrons bearing the tri-crossed blades of a Gosdan.

Vilas glared across the short distance between

them.

"Gosdan," Radiant Tano said, taking a knee before rising. "The Beast of Khiya will assist, having agreed to all conditions."

Machical glanced up at Vilas with a faint sneer. "Agreeing and doing are two separate things."

"They are," Vilas replied, speaking evenly with some effort. *I will be damned if I let him spoil my revenge – and he is only* one *part.*

The general grunted. "You haven't changed. Still a bitter loser."

Loser? As though war and life and death were a blasted *game*? Vilas clenched his hands. A pig of a man, no, someone *barely* a man stood before him, entirely the same in character, if not appearance. "But you have changed."

"Time passes for some, Maelohas."

He gestured to the road, where its perfectly interlocking stones ran in a mighty line through lush, rolling plains. Vague shapes of travellers approaching dotted the highway. "The rest of my force is meeting us with the mounts. We're proceeding on foot." One of the other soldiers sighed, only faintly, but the general turned. "You had better not be complaining about a little walking, boy."

He stiffened. "No, Gosdan."

"Had you not all missed the morning's training, you wouldn't have to do this."

"Yes, Gosdan."

The general waved them along the highway, then took a position at the head of the group.

Out of sight, for the moment. *Good.*

Vilas followed from where he walked in the centre of a handful of Radiants and the ten soldiers, their matching armour bright beneath the sun. It could have been a festival, if he wanted to pretend his escort was part of a little parade…

…or whatever it took to actually suppress a trembling need to lash out at them.

He relaxed his jaw and drew in a long breath.

Control is vital. Vital.

Though tension still ran through his body, it was tempered by a welcome surprise. Outside the city, a somehow boundless quality to the very air struck him, echoed in the rising scent of grass and flowers, the vastness of the sky too. How very *above* it seemed now, that crucial sense of space. How stunning. The world was a stretching place after all.

After decades within his cell, how easy it had been to forget, and how welcome that such a fact soothed his rage better than expected.

Have I missed it this much?

Even when passing modest shrines with their lattice of crossed palings, tips painted yellow and supposedly used to capture the mischievous *kikena*, even something so mundane being used to mark smaller roads that would lead eventually to farmhouses, was enough to drive home just how many steps he could take without running into a wall.

An actual taste of freedom.

"Don't expect any of this to last, Maelohas." Machical spoke from his position ahead without looking at Vilas; instead, the man's gaze was fixed upon the highway.

"Shut up, Onathian." It was difficult to keep his words calm. "I am trying to enjoy the scenery."

"Listen. Keep that tongue of yours still, or I'll finish what I started in the war."

Vilas shook his head. "Are you an imbecile?"

The general came to a halt, spinning on his heel. "What?"

"Killing me is hardly permitted by your queen."

"Bah, I'm warning you!" Machical gripped the hilt of his longsword. The scabbard had been decorated with disused Onathian runes, which amounted to little more than boasting. His arm was trembling and his second, a tall fellow, moved closer.

Radiant Tano himself stepped before the Gosdan, hands raised. "Please, we must focus on the path ahead."

"Since you are no match for the Brutes," Vilas said with his own glare, "you should listen to the Radiant."

"Are *you* a match for them?" the Gosdan snapped.

"I need to be alive to find out, don't I? So give up the posturing as 'Hero of Onath' and follow your queen's orders." His tone was still even. He'd mastered his fury; and a cool head suited just about every situation, not in the least for those that dealt in life and death. Rejecting an urge to snap back had another benefit, too. It caused the Gosdan to grow more agitated.

"Posturing? Posturing?"

"Always," Vilas said, glaring now. "Or do all heroes lock school children in burning buildings?"

Machical's second gave his superior a look of doubt.

The general snarled, shoving the man away as he pointed a trembling finger at Vilas. "You will not besmirch my name."

Vilas folded his arms. "If you aren't going to use this time to tell me anything useful, then don't speak to me at all."

Machical seemed to be trying to avoid biting through his tongue, but he spun on a heel and strode on without answering. Muttering and glances from his soldiers followed. Of course, none did much but glare, since that was all they were permitted. *Surprising that no-one has lashed out at me yet.*

"What of you, Radiant Tano?" Vilas asked. "Where are the Cherished Sons now? Will Machical even allow me to examine the Brute's hand?"

"I imagine so," he replied as he scratched at his beard, his gaze disapproving. "Once we reach the camp, I'm sure he'll have calmed down – no thanks to you. And the Cherished Sons are due east of here. The hills of Prianolam."

"I see." Vilas turned to the east, where a faint haze of wood-smoke in the air above the plain suggested a village or hamlet. Beyond that in turn would be the hills of Prianolam, at least, according to his collection of maps. And his memory of them. More important, perhaps, was the 'scarred nation' of Devonas beyond. *Old enemies of Onath, hungry to sow dissent?* "Are they receiving weapons from Devonas? Assuming the Sons cannot source them here. Or perhaps... pirates supplying from the River Midon?"

"Probably. The cultists we intercepted were not very forthcoming," Tano said, and something that could have been distaste entered his voice. "Nor did they live long."

"Suicide?"

"They carried something within their stomachs, we believe. Once they were captured, it was not long before they curled up into corpses."

"No clues?"

"There *is* a Western woman in the camp," he replied. "But even so, doesn't that ignore the very real evidence of Brutes?"

"The more I know, the better chance I have of coming to a decision on whether the Brutes are involved. Or if they have even *returned*."

"You doubt our word?"

"There's no reason to discard a plot by Davorians. Or perhaps the Cherished Sons are simply now more sophisticated than I remember," he replied with a shrug. "There is even a possibility the Brutes *have* returned but are allied with or being used by others. I do not mean to close off any avenue of possibility."

"Very well."

Vilas stretched both arms before him, hands linked, and his fingers cracked. "Our numbers? Theirs?"

"Two score, counting you," he replied. "The Cherished Sons perhaps three score."

A little more than expected. But still not a problem for a Pentagal of Radiants or the army either, had they been sent forth... "Then here is what I should have asked before. *How* does the queen expect us to learn the truth about the Brutes? If the cult is slaughtered, or manages to kill itself off, then we discover nothing. The paint is of note, I have no problem admitting that much, but it's not proof alone. It would be just as useful to wait and watch, to find the source of the weapon supply."

"When it comes to watching, we have done as much," Tano replied. "Nothing yet. The queen expects you to see some evidence, one way or another, whenever we attack. Should it come to this, there is a trail to follow left by the Brute, and you will protect me and Yadira on that path, if we're attacked."

Of course, the Steel Maiden. "So, she is meeting us at the camp?"

"Yes," Tano replied, and something flickered across his face, some emotion that was immediately controlled. Vilas could have sighed. The lad remained difficult to read. "You will meet her soon enough." Tano gestured ahead, to a crest in the highway, where a small group of soldiers waited.

A single Radiant stood to the fore, white clothing

luminous beneath the sun. A row of mounts waited beyond in turn, concealing any others that might have travelled with the Radiant, but there were certainly enough animals for those who left the city to also ride comfortably.

Vilas glanced at the line of horses, their dark coats gleaming. One shook its head, flicking a dark mane. Did they actually seem taller than those from decades ago? *And do I remember how to ride?* He nearly chuckled; finding out might just be fun.

Chapter 4.

Outside, wind and dust hurled itself against the tent walls as Vilas peered down at the Brute's tattooed hand. Prone upon the table, it was a grey and black hunk coloured by spiralling ink – ink that stood far too strong in its orange and thinner lines of blue.

"This would be difficult to fake," Vilas said. "Our paints and inks are not so vivid."

Tano and Machical stood beside him; the younger man's expression one of concern, but the Gosdan's impatience flowed from his folded arms and roving gaze. His eyes were bright beneath additional lamps placed within the tent, in turn illuminating the dark blue of the flaps.

"Care to tell us anything we haven't already ascertained?" the Gosdan asked.

Vilas glared across the table. "I promise not to kill you the moment I am free, if you shut your mouth. Now get out and let me focus."

Machical's eyes widened. He snatched at his hilt once more, but this time Tano caught the man's arm. "My Lord, please think of the people."

The general shoved Tano aside and stormed from the tent without a word. Something crashed to the earth after – a stand of weapons? A brazier? *No matter, just so long as he is furious.*

Tano was shaking his head. "I understand there is an unpleasant history between you both, but that seems a foolish course of action. We must depend on each other in order to save the city. If nothing else, you mean to honour your word to Her Majesty, do you not?"

Vilas glanced up from the hunk of hand – the brute's appendage was missing two fingers, but it was no clever fakery. That much had been clear the moment he laid eyes upon it. "Do you have family, Lord Tano?"

He hesitated, perhaps thrown by the change in topic. "I do. My sister and mother."

"Then you do not understand at all," Vilas said as he waved the Radiant closer. "Now. Tell me, what do you see here, in the palm?" There was a very specific detail that could have been overlooked, an important detail, too.

Tano muttered beneath his breath but moved closer.

Aside from calluses on the granite *texture* of its skin, the cuts and bruising, abyssal-dark blood dried and flaking, there was a row of small puncture marks. Inside one puncture, something tiny glimmered in pink – something anyone ought to have noticed on close examination.

After a moment, it seemed Tano was about to pull back, but he stopped. "Do you mean the punctures?"

"I do. The second to last one."

Tano squinted. "Is it a petal?"

"I don't think so." He lifted the small belt knife from where it rested on the table beside a hammer and chisel, and used the tip of the blade to free a fragment of smooth stone – it clicked faintly across the tabletop, a milky pink that gleamed in the lamp-light. *As I thought.* "This is interesting."

"Is it?"

"Yes. It is not quartz, nor a precious gem – yet look at the colour and the texture."

"Smooth enough to come from the ocean."

Vilas nodded. "Or one other place. North of here, high in the Otakom Mountains by a dark lake, the walls feature stone like this."

"Are you saying you saw traces of the Brutes there?"

"I *have* been to Lake Sirathemon but I did not see any traces. It is said they... holidayed there, long, long ago." Or so Jiana had always claimed in her stories about them. *And hadn't Grandmother said something similar?*

Tano frowned. "That sounds like you're telling me the Brutes... travelled for leisure. Or change. And not simply to find food or to ravage new lands."

"That might be beyond the bounds of my task, as given by the queen," he replied, but still gestured to the pink stone. "All I can say for certain is that Lake Sirathemon is worth investigating, if the truth about the Brutes is important."

"Of course it is," the Radiant replied. "But Gosdan Machical will decide our course. And we are far closer to the Cherished Sons."

"So we are." And it probably did not matter. The lake was not going to disappear. "How near are we to their lair now?"

Tano moved to a nearby pack and rummaged around, withdrawing a long leather tube with glass set in each end. A curious item. "There is a vantage point not far from here that we can use."

Vilas smiled. "Tactically sound. And diplomatic."

"Diplomatic?"

"No need to act modest – it's an obvious but smart decision nonetheless."

"I am not certain I follow."

"Of course you do. Keeping me away from your leader while he cools off. It's perfectly sound and I have neither the willingness nor the capacity to refuse, if you wanted to force me."

The Radiant raised an eyebrow. "Then you will no longer antagonise him?"

"I promise no such thing."

"That is foolishness. I had not expected the legacy of the Maelohas to be a child trapped within a man's body." The fellow was glaring but did not make any threatening move – nor did he need to, since using the collar would be far easier.

"Disappointments in life are plentiful," Vilas replied. "And I will deliver more, I am certain of that." For all Tano's composure, the Radiant was still young and staying in control for each and every moment was an arduous skill to learn – it wasn't difficult to understand the young man's frustration. He probably expected the Beast of Khiya to turn the coming tide, if such a tide existed. The lad truly cared for the city – admirable, certainly, but a doomed hope. *Especially considering what I will do when I am free.* "I'm offering my cooperation; we all know I want my freedom. The Gosdan is not so green as to anger his queen by slaughtering me."

"Given your infamous oath, you will understand if my doubts persist."

"Yes, but my oath is specific – it was 'by my hand', if you remember the words."

Tano did not answer, only shook his head.

"I am not toying with you, Radiant."

"No?"

"No. If I were to sabotage the queen's efforts here, and through my inaction let the dam break and ravage the city, that would offer me no satisfaction at all." And it was no lie. It *had* to be with his own hands. "I will destroy Onath myself and permit no other to come even close before me."

The Radiant narrowed his eyes, staring for a long moment. "Follow me, then." He started toward the exit then paused, glancing over his shoulder. "And I offer an oath of my own, Beast. Will you bear witness?"

Interesting. "Do so."

"The moment My Queen grants your freedom, I will take your life. For the sake of my honour, I'm giving this warning."

The Radiant left the tent.

Vilas followed with a small smile. *I think I'm starting to like this boy.*

Chapter 5.

Vilas glanced back down the twisting trail, frowning at a hint of movement in the afternoon shadows. Something shifted between the pine needles, and it wasn't the wind. Merely a bird? The squad had been somewhat raucous on the climb up into the hills. *As though something startled them perhaps.*

"Are we being followed?" Tano asked from where he knelt before a row of shrubs, their purple leaves almost black on the underside.

"Likely birds only."

The Radiant paused, 'spyglass' in hand – the item from the tent was not a weapon, but an invention from distant lands. Apparently, sailors were all using them now, and the glass allowed a person to see distant objects as though they were close. "I will watch the back trail while you use this."

Vilas accepted the invention then knelt within the shrubs, using the spyglass to part the branches. Far below, the curve of dry hills half-concealed a bustling, barricaded camp of people in orange or blue tunics. They worked before a large cave opening to reinforce a wall of stone.

Could the Brutes actually be waiting in the darkness?

Even with the evidence back in the Machical's camp, it didn't seem likely.

Some of the Cherished Sons worked with picks and shovels, deepening trenches across the entry to the camp too – at least a score of them.

Farther in, another score of men were split evenly between those carrying armloads of spears or quivers into the cave, and a group that was seated. Those were gathered beneath a figure that stood tall upon a crate.

The cultists were too distant for much more to be revealed... and so Vilas finally lifted the smaller end of the spyglass to his eye and closed the other, blinking to adjust to the sharpened points of the palisade, now so close that he could make out tool-marks in the wood. "I see."

Vilas moved the glass slowly up and across the camp; now frowns and smiles were visible, the colour of blonde and brown hair and beards, even orange and blue paint on some faces and arms, along with a symbol – a curved line within a second, larger line – which sat on their chests.

So too, more detail on their weapons: swords, bows and spears, all seeming of good quality. *Just who is funding them?* Someone was paying for the tunics and weapons. And the provisions too. Especially such expensive paint. That alone was the largest clue. *It's something for the rich to toy around with, after all.*

Not a resource to be wasted on military efforts, let alone by aping a long dead race.

While the Cherished Sons definitely seemed to have grown in number from what he was expecting, and even more could well lurk within the unknown cave, the fools were still not a force to threaten the city. Not in any way.

Vilas moved the spyglass slowly, and this time stopped on the speaker – a somewhat delicate-looking man. His blond hair was slicked back from his forehead, a plaited beard tied with dark thread, his eyes alight as he spoke. The passion of his words was clear, even through the spyglass, but it wasn't a mindless fervour.

Or at least, it didn't seem to be from afar.

Hmmm. Foolish to make any premature decisions about the man, leader or no. *Even so, duping humans is one thing, but could he really have convinced Brutes to join his cause?*

Vilas lowered the tool, then stopped.

Wait...

He swung the glass back to the leader, who seemed to have paused on a presumably salient point, arms outstretched, sleeves trailing, but there, leaning against the supply crates was a woman with the distinctive clothing of a Davorian – the dark fur over a shirt that left her midriff bare, she was indeed more accustomed to the warmer clime of her home.

The woman watched on with a satisfied expression, her mouth set in a faint smile. Unlike the travellers Vilas recalled from his youth, this Davorian wore tiny skulls in her pierced ears. Carved from bone? *Don't the Davorians consider burial sacred?* "No bones should be woken from their sleep by the cruel light of day," he murmured, fairly certain he had their proverb correct.

Even from the ridge where Vilas was hidden, there seemed to be something… off about the Davorian when he focused on her gaze. Her eyes were a little too wide for her seemingly relaxed pose...

"What of the Davorian woman?" Vilas asked, speaking over his shoulder.

"She is rarely seen and she does not often speak herself, at least not that we have observed."

"You mean she doesn't address the members?"

"Hardly even the leader himself. We cannot watch them every moment, however."

Vilas frowned. "I won't guess at motivations here, but what else have you learnt about Davorian involvement?"

"It has been discussed, but the incident at the Sky Mines was so long ago. They haven't even been seen this far east in perhaps five years. The woman may simply be a concubine."

The history Vilas knew, which made the woman's presence even more reason for concern – even beyond comparatively recent reluctance for Davorians to leave their borders. "Then, am I to believe that she is merely a single discontent from afar, joined with other malcontents by happenstance, sharing the bed of their leader? For me, that does not explain her presence."

"We do not know either way."

"What of the leader?"

"Lefios. Former city marksman. No-one is certain why he joined the Cherished Sons, but he deposed their leader within a month of joining, some years ago now. We have gathered only a few more details about him."

"Few?"

"I assume my superiors never deemed them any kind of threat before recent times."

"Perhaps a fair assumption. The queen mentioned the drawing of unhappy youths?"

"He preaches about injustice and blames the nobles and Radiants or corrupt officials for all the ills facing the city."

"Well, he's not a complete fool, then," Vilas said.

Tano frowned. "Meaning what, precisely?"

"A discussion for another time. If then," Vilas replied. "Has anyone attempted to infiltrate the cult, or at least get a look inside the cavern?"

"The Gosdan has been waiting on you for such a task. What we have learnt is mostly by taking the Sons from the city streets, or observation here."

"Waiting for me in case they actually have Brutes

inside?"

"I believe so, yes."

Vilas handed back the spyglass. "What of you, Tano? Do you believe there are actually Brutes hidden inside the cavern?"

The Radiant drew in a breath. "Not inside, no."

"And the corpse?"

"Something the Sons found and copied patterns from," he said. "Where the Brute itself came from in the first place, well, that I could not guess."

"You may discover the truth soon enough."

"How so?"

"Because of this." Vilas tapped his collar. "If Machical sends me inside, you're the one who will have to follow. They will expect you to control my power, of course."

"Yes. Of course."

"Are you ready for that? In the past, many have suffered."

"I am aware of the trials undertaken to properly control you." Tano's expression remained unperturbed.

"Good. Then I expect you to deliver me exactly as much power as I request. *Instantly*. Because if there is another Brute inside, or more than one, then hesitation will kill me, you, the Gosdan and everyone in the city."

"That I know," Tano said with a nod that revealed nothing about his feelings at such a likelihood and instead, suggested an unwavering sense of duty.

Chapter 6.

The Steel Maiden, Yadira, stood at the edge of the now-bustling camp as the evening meal was prepared, helm beneath her arm, silver breastplate, greaves and gauntlets covered in engravings of birds – talons and wings, mostly, but beaks and eyes were visible too. A mighty wingspan covered her breastplate, the feathers differentiated by depth of stroke, as if to represent two colours.

It marked her as akin to local nobility, only in the northern mountains of Eami, her role was closer to protector rather than leech. A true Servant of the People. At least, so it had been for Steel Maidens in the past.

Blue-black hair streamed free, motionless in the still dusk where she looked over the camp, unaware of his approach. From one wrist hung a leather strap and a sword with a curved hilt was belted at her side.

No hint of the Steel Maiden's famous magical

speed where she waited – yet why would there be? And even if the stories were exaggerations, if nothing else, she seemed absolutely more than capable at first glance.

When the woman turned to face them, her expression could not be described as welcoming – concealed as it was beneath a half-mask, shaped as a falcon's face. Only her mouth and eyes were visible, pale blue eyes expectant.

"This is the Steel Maiden, Yadira,"Tano said, offering her a half-bow. "She is Damijir among her people. Not unlike a Lord or Lady here."

He nodded. "I am aware of Eami hierarchy, Tano."

"Beast of Khiya," Yadira said, her voice deeper than expected. She bore no trace of any Eamis accent, suggesting either great skill with language or a long stay in the city of Onath, perhaps. She stepped closer. "I am pleased to have you join us. I trust we can cooperate to uncover the truth behind this new threat."

"As my reputation has reached you, you must be aware that I seek my freedom and my revenge above all else."

"I do," she replied with a nod, and her gaze softened. "Your bitterness and grief pours forth."

Vilas frowned. "I hope you're not expecting an apology for that."

"Not at all. And I hope to help you, even in a small way, while we travel together."

Vilas regarded her a moment... was she sincere? She was. How odd. "Well, I will keep my word and deal with the Brutes first."

"That is pleasing to hear," she replied. "But I must now risk offence and ask about your cursed power. Are the Bindings of the Radiants enough to contain even you?"

Tano cleared his throat. "Lady Yadira, the collar does control him."

She nodded. "So you and your general have promised, Radiant Tano."

"I appreciate your own forthrightness, Steel Maiden." Vilas turned to leave. "Would one of you send someone to find me when Machical is ready to make a decision about the Cherished Sons?"

He'd not managed to reach the main tent, where someone ought to have been able to direct him to his own lodgings, when a new voice called.

"I'm ready now."

Gosdan Machical stood with a pack slung across one armoured shoulder. His face was twisted into a glare – the same old glare beneath all the wrinkles and white hair, right down to his eyebrows.

Tano and the Steel Maiden hurried after as Vilas gestured back to the command tent. "And what have you decided to do about the mystery of the Brute?"

"You've seen the cultists' camp now?"

"I have. Fortified, their true number concealed by the cave. Even so, no real threat to the army. The Davorian woman?"

"Not alone, as it turns out."

Tano straightened. "My Lord?"

"A small force with the look of Davorian mercenaries has been seen to the north. We'll be intercepting them immediately," he replied. "The woman and that traitor Lefios need to be dealt with too, but the priority is discovering more about the links to Devonas first."

"And the Wahkyog?" Vilas asked.

The general said only, "Second priority."

"Contrary to the queen's orders."

"Listen for a damnable moment. One may well lead to the other, can't you see even that much? Historical hunting grounds lie between here and Devonas, don't they? Not that I owe a novelty like you an explanation, but I won't be ignoring such a lead."

"Novelty?" A new barb from the man. *Not precisely inaccurate either.* But perhaps 'pet' of the monarchy would have been closer to the truth. "No doubt I am for some of the younger ones here. But you remember what I am capable of."

"Yes. And once you've outlived your usefulness, I will deal with you. That is my promise, Maelohas."

"I see," Vilas replied. "What about before then? Are you planning to divide your forces here?"

"Reinforcements are coming," the man replied with a grunt. "I will strike the mercenaries while Sergeant Chada will be waiting for any rats to flee east. Tano will take you and the Eamis into the mountains at dawn. Find whatever you can and report back. If the Brutes *have* actually returned, do not engage. We need information. Is that clear?"

"I see. Only Tano and Yadira as minders. Interesting."

"Radiant Tano will keep a close hold on that collar, don't worry," the man said with a leering grin – a disgustingly familiar grin. "I think even you will be surprised at his strength."

Not likely. "And where is my tent, then?"

Machical pointed to a small tent of dark blue, not too far from the command post.

Vilas strode across a patch of muddy grass and climbed inside his shelter, ignoring a pack of provisions and settling onto the bedroll with a soft groan. He stared up at the roof. *Stupid to be so tired, you're not old yet.* A small tear in the tent's fabric had been sewn together with some care, and he continued to stare as he lifted a hand and let his fingers trail across his collar, counting the grooves. A reminder that, despite the rarity of time spent beyond the city – time spent *outside* – he was still a prisoner.

It was more than a way to limit the Embers of Maelohas. Among other feats, the collar could guide others to his location if he ran; it was quite impressive magic – right down to its form. The silver was not so tight that it restricted his movement or breathing on a day-to-day basis, light enough that it was possible... sometimes, for short periods, to forget he wore it.

Or, even forget that it had been forced upon him by Onathian hands.

And I bled so much, back then.

Would traces of dried blood still linger beneath the silver, decades later? Fanciful. But closing his eyes, it was no trouble to imagine a slickness to his skin, a slickness that coated the mineral that contained him.

Perhaps most galling were the half-dozen seams that could be traced; sharp, square lines. A similar pattern to those used by the Radiants for their bindings, of course. And the suggestion that each seam represented a weakness — a way to freedom — that was cruellest of all.

None were openings.

At least, not according to my hands.

"But one day, that won't matter," he muttered.

Not if his research proved accurate. He rolled onto his side then, letting a small smile keep him company until sleep followed.

Chapter 7.

The muted light of dawn cast the trail in deep shadows, highlights of grey visible upon the edges of all that lay before them – stone, trunk, and branch alike. Even the dark lumps of pinecones, where they seemed to push through the bedding of needles. Small flowers peeked from beneath furry plants that sometimes extended across the trail, their colours pale suggestions only.

"Do not fall behind, Vilas." Radiant Tano's voice carried down from farther up the trail.

Vilas turned away from their backtrail, where below, the empty Radiant camp waited. Questions lingered. What links, if any, would Machical find to the Brutes? The likelihood should have been similar to discovering gold in the sky. But the Davorians were not sneaking around the hills for no reason.

Will we fare any better beyond the dam?

He quickened his stride, muttering to himself about having their horses taken by the general. When he caught up with Tano and Steel Maiden Yadira, the two were speaking of the Brutes themselves.

"Then they did not cross the sea at any time?" the Radiant was asking.

"Not according to our histories," she said. "Yet there is a part of me that wishes to face one."

Tano blinked. "You do?"

"Of course," she said with a nod. "You should understand, seeing you are among the strongest of the Radiants, after all."

"Are you suggesting that no human would pose you a challenge?"

"Some would, of course," she said with a smile, and her eyes were glittering behind the falcon mask. "But to face such a mighty creature, that would be a true test of my will."

"Is that why you are assisting Queen Ima?" Vilas asked.

"No, Beast of Khiya. It is not only a diplomatic honour, but a responsibility. Our two nations continue to stand together against those who would bear us ill, of course."

"Address me as 'Vilas' while we travel together," he said with a frown.

She glanced to Tano, who nodded.

Vilas narrowed his eyes. *Does he actually believe his role includes granting permission in matters regarding how I'm to be referred?*

"Certainly, Vilas," she said.

Vilas raised a hand. "Ridiculous. No. Not under such conditions. Call me what you will, but do not use my name if only because you have decided that I am the property of the Onathians, and that you therefore require their permission to do so."

"I apologise. I was unsure of your pride regarding the name."

He slowed. "Do you... think I am *proud* of that day?"

"I do not know. It seemed the most formal option, considering my people know little of the Maelohas."

Tano came to a halt. "You need not be so thorny. I only sought to guide her in terms of etiquette."

"Is that so?"

Yadira gestured to the collar. "Again, forgive my ignorance, but is that not the nature of your situation? That he would grant permission?"

"The nature of my situation is that only *I* can stand against the Brutes. Therefore you, Tano here, and the entire city of Onath remain at my mercy. All are depending on me, and as much as I desire freedom, I can afford to be very patient."

"And what do you mean by that?" Tano demanded. "Are you saying that you would potentially let the Brutes destroy the city, and what... gamble on your long lifespan?"

"No. Again, you are forgetting my oath. The city must fall by my hand, Radiant," he replied, with a deep frown. "But I am under no obligation to save any particular individual. I'm sure the queen and your general have plenty of lackeys they might send along to help me."

He folded his arms. "You're wasting your breath if you mean to antagonise me. I know you wish to succeed, Vilas. Especially considering your immoral arrangement with Her Majesty."

"Obviously, the *city* at least must survive long enough for me to keep my oath and for the queen to do the same."

"There is another, hidden agreement?" Yadira asked. "I was told he would fight for his freedom."

"Yes," Tano said, but did not elaborate, instead glaring at Vilas. "I believe that you will do your utmost to stop the Brutes, if only to prevent them beating you to your own revenge, exactly as you have promised. But you will not lay a finger upon the queen while I draw breath."

"Certainly."

The Steel Maiden was frowning now. "What is this other agreement?"

Tano resumed walking. "We should continue."

Yadira glanced after but did not follow. "He claimed it was immoral."

"I will share her bed if I save the city."

"Ah. Then perhaps I should continue to address you as 'Beast', after all," Yadira said as she too, resumed the climb up the trail. "Or perhaps you are more pitiful than I imagined."

"Pitiful?"

"Yes. You are using desire to mask your pain." Her tone had been matter of fact. It was difficult to be certain, but she did not seem to be concerned with the arrangement in the same manner as Tano. Was it actually for what she considered to be his suffering? If true, were all Steel Maidens so… conscientious? *Unlikely.*

Vilas trailed his minders at a distance, though they were rarely out of sight, not when dark needles of the pines covered the climb, nor when the trail wound around the sides of a steep gorge.

Only by noon did he actually rejoin them to remove plain provisions from his pack, where he chewed in silence.

A silence that was entirely pleasant.

Time to soak in the sweet scent of pine needles. And to let bird song wash over him; the birds were mostly happy it seemed, though a few were obviously screeching rather than singing.

And so the rest of the afternoon passed, his feet, legs and back soon aching. Far too long since he'd worked so hard – and only from walking! It was a climb to reach the pass and the dam, but the trail wasn't so steep as it wound up. *Merchant wagons manage this path without any trouble – I have grown softer.*

But changed or not, he had no trouble helping to set up camp.

Each tent was placed at an equal distance from

the other, facing the firepit where water boiled, the warm scent of spiced meat rising from the pot. *And we've arranged things this way because it is... what? A simple desire for space? Or distrust?* During the meal, conversation remained focused on the dam. By noon tomorrow they would reach the site, where Tano would once again question the guards and engineers, mostly for the benefit of Vilas and Yadira.

Then, it would probably be necessary to follow the river farther north.

Eventually, perhaps, to Lake Sirathemon where the pink stone could be found. Whether that would lead to more evidence of the Brutes? Impossible to say.

After their meal, it was Tano who broke the silence. "Despite what I have seen, I wonder how a single, isolated Brute could survive so long."

"Do you mean undetected?" Vilas asked.

"Partly."

"We knew them as long-lived, just as we are, for one."

Yadira frowned as she spoke. "If they have survived in numbers, would even someone with your power be able to defeat such foes?"

Vilas spread his hands. "That depends on how much Tano grants me."

"Then the collar can be adjusted in some way? I am curious, since I understand it is unusual, even among the Radiants?"

Tano nodded. "The Binding-Collar *is* quite unusual. The surviving Luminaries argue amongst themselves whether it is the most precious item yet created, in part due to its flexibility as a tool and as a collar, but also because it can even contain the Embers of a Maelohas."

"*The* Maeloha," Vilas added. "Since I am the last."

"Yes."

Vilas continued. "Since we are, at least ostensibly, working together now, why not explain for Yadira's benefit?"

"Indeed. It's probably best to describe the collar as offering distinct stages of constraint – six Bindings. The same way that I can manipulate the hidden ties that hold things together, I can lessen the bindings the collar has placed on Vilas' power, a little at a time."

"Those established by your Elders, the Luminaries?"

"Yes. Six Bindings to completely contain him."

"Hmmm." Yadira glanced between them. "I understand what you have said but it is not easy to place into context. Have any ever estimated how many Bindings it would have taken to prevent the destruction at Darkmoor, for instance?"

"Well..."

"Three," Vilas replied. He could have smiled when he said it, considering the shock on her face, but there was no joy to be taken from such a grave day. Regrettable in a way that was similar but distinct to the destruction of Khiya. Only a hollowness within now, that once more expanded from within his chest, pushing outward, applying pressure upon his ribcage, his tendons and skin. "Perhaps you also have a clearer understanding of why, should *many* Brutes have survived, that I am the only one who can save the city."

Worry glimmered in her eyes. "Somewhat. Even so, at what cost? Would the Brutes and we ourselves, the very mountains around us, survive such a clash?"

"Do not worry," he replied. "I can control the Embers. And if by chance I fail to do so, then any Radiant can cut off my access via the collar and the agony it offers."

"Then the Radiants have obviously tested re-applying the Bindings after they've been released?"

Tano nodded. "Queen Ima would not have presented her idea otherwise."

"Tested to three, at least," Vilas added.

Long ago, it had been. Or, somehow only two decades... such tests had indeed proven that the strongest among the Radiants could successfully reapply three Bindings, once those three had been released.

No-one had ever sought to remove four Bindings during their trials, of course, not even the Luminaries.

Queen Ima, Gosdan Machical, Radiant Tano and anyone else involved in the effort to discover the truth behind the Wahkyog corpse, were no doubt all hoping that there would never be a need to discover what releasing four or five let alone all six Bindings would mean.

And above all, it seemed they hoped if such a day came to pass, Tano could re-apply them. *The strongest amongst them.*

Before the matter with the Brutes was resolved, that fact would have to be tested.

Chapter 8.

Churning water echoed alongside the road the next morning, a restless language that filled even the branches above. It grew especially agitated as rapids tumbled along frequent falls, as the Lidasch River charged down toward the distant city. At times, the riverbed lay far enough below them, winking up from the bottom of the gorge, that a stumble and fall from the road would easily kill.

Or shatter a body into a sack of broken... everything. *Long-lived or not, I won't survive that.*

At other times, Vilas had only to take a few steps from the carefully paved road they travelled in order to plunge his water-flask beneath the cool surface, the clean scent of minerals something he paused to savour with each moment.

Sometimes, the water seemed touched by the chill of ice, or the scent of pine too – here, the Lidasch's voice hushed to a sweet murmur.

Beautiful.

Letting your imagination run away, again?

Before noon, the fearsome walls of the dam slid into view between the trees. It appeared almost a mountain itself, splitting the dark of the Otakom Ranges with smooth bluestone.

Supposedly constructed last century by one of the old Kings, it had been reinforced by Radiant Bindings – bindings which, up until now, no-one had seemed concerned over.

But the Brute's corpse had changed that.

It is *a mighty structure. But the real threat would come from occupation by a hostile force.* Led by the Brutes or not, if someone overwhelmed the guard and attendants, and opened the flow gates or sabotaged them somehow, the city would be under serious threat.

Providing the attackers could unravel the Bindings.

But if they could somehow *destroy* the dam from within... He narrowed his eyes. A good method, yes. *But how much satisfaction could I actually take from that?* Striking a blow from such a distance, being absent for the actual destruction of Onath?

No. *Inadequate.*

At present, the gates were only partially open, like mighty teeth, with water plummeting down to the river in frenzied white, the spray drifting toward his vantage point upon the breeze.

The Steel Maiden stared up at the monstrous feat of construction with one hand on her hip. "How would even Brutes hope to destroy something like this?"

"Perhaps they can break through the stone," Tano replied. "We don't know for sure. But any humans would attack that chamber." He pointed to the dam's peak. There, built as if it were moulded, and half-protruding from the wall, a dome with a narrow row of windows sat. A viewing platform had been built beneath but was not accessible from the ground.

Instead, a long stair with a gleaming handrail climbed up, cut into the mountain, disappearing into the wall itself near the top.

Vilas ran a hand through his hair. A tedious amount of steps, yes, but the dam and its chamber would be accessible from level-ground to the north also, from the 'top', basically. *So not too difficult, at all.*

And the Brutes themselves, if they had returned en masse… was everyone underestimating them?

Legends described immense strength, yes, but that was not all – simply one threat among the many. Stone-like skin and corrosive blood. And something else. *Mother mentioned the five dangers of the Wahkyog, hadn't she?*

Either the fall at the dam was unrelated or something had gone wrong with the Davorians trying to control the creatures… assuming they could be controlled. "I want to speak to whoever found the pieces of the corpse. Have they been watching the area surrounding the dam?"

"I would be surprised if they hadn't," Tano replied as

he led them toward the stair where it cut deep into the mountain, enough to provide shelter from rain, if not storms.

At the foot of the steps, a heavy gate swung open, a single Radiant waiting beyond. He was young – younger than Tano – and blinked at the sight of Vilas and the Steel Maiden, mostly focusing on Yadira. "Ah, welcome to Otakom Pass Dam. I am Radiant Risi and I will guide you."

Tano made introductions, and the younger fellow then switched his wide gaze to Vilas.

"Yes, I am the Beast of Khiya. What can you tell us about the Brute?"

"Well…" He glanced to Tano, who nodded.

"Not all that much… sir," he said, stumbling over the honorific. "But I can take you to Mira. She will be able to answer your questions, I'm sure. Please, follow me."

Radiant Risi started up the steps, his robe darkening within the shade.

It did not take long for Vilas' legs to begin to ache once more, and he found himself not exactly falling behind but not keeping pace either. And while the others spoke as they walked, Yadira with barely any trouble even in her armour, for Vilas only the roar of the water kept him company.

By the time they finally reached the top, the roar had dulled a little. He gripped the rail to catch his breath, staring down to the distant riverbed where the churn eventually evened out into a clear blue lake, narrowing quickly to a broad river, the tranquil view ringed by treetops. *Quite a drop.*

"Sir Vilas?"

Their guide waited at an open door of steel. Tano was already passing through, Yadira close behind. The Radiant's back was quite straight, and his shoulders seemed to relax as he entered the building.

"No titles necessary, Risi." Vilas quickened his step and joined them within the dam walls, finding a corridor of dark stone similar to that of the palace. Evenly spaced lamps were just as pale. More noteworthy were the occasional alcoves with small, square panels of steel.

The same pattern continued for some time, unbroken by window, painting or plant. Eventually, Vilas slowed to examine one of the panels, and Radiant Risi smiled. "This is one of but many more. They allow us to monitor the Bindings on the dam from any floor. Ah, not that any are in danger of weakening, exactly."

Impressive. "What do you mean by 'exactly'?"

"It cannot be denied that Otakom Dam is one of the oldest structures within the kingdom, and of course, no Binding lasts forever..." he trailed off at the sound of a pair of footsteps from around the corner.

A man and a woman appeared, each dressed in plain clothing of a dark hue, arms laden with strips of steel. They passed with nods of deference to Tano first, and then Risi, but did not speak.

Why had the young man halted his explanation?

It was no secret that Bindings faded after significant timespans, but that was why Radiants strengthened them. *Is he afraid to reveal something?*

Vilas did not press the young man. Tano waved them over to where he now stood at a guarded door. More heavy steel and, no doubt, this would have been also set with Bindings.

But the guards admitted them without use of their gift, revealing a spacious, domed room. The long bank of narrow windows admitted plenty of light, allowing a perfect vantage of the lake and river below.

A chamber for Binding.

More panels of steel were arranged on either side of enormous levers, along with gleaming hook-like tools and seating. The rest of the dome featured storage cupboards and in one corner, tables and chairs – all very regular. One doorway led to another room, and perhaps the opposite end of the dam wall, along with a set of stairs near yet more levers that presumably led to the viewing ledge.

Only two figures stood inside, both older men. One, a Radiant in white, his silvery hair matched by rings upon his fingers. The other man seemed to be an attendant. He was dressed in a similar fashion to those Vilas had passed in the corridor. His bald head gleamed beneath the windows' light, and while he smiled in greeting, the Radiant only addressed Tano.

"Welcome, Radiant. I trust you will have no objection to being shown directly to Captain Mira?

I am sure you will want to continue your most urgent task immediately."

"Of course, Radiant," Tano replied.

"Risi, take them to the barracks. I believe you will find her there."

Vilas shook his head as they were led almost immediately back into the corridors, where the small group then wound its way up and out of the dam wall and outside to a large, open-air section of the Otakom Dam.

The space was still contained by broad paving stones, and ringed by twin barracks featuring brickwork of a uniform size – these buildings were connected by a broad bridge across the water. *Splitting the defences, I see.* The stone bridge spanned the expanse of the Lidasch River, a glittering beast of a lake whose impenetrable depths bore an expectant air.

Perhaps having the barracks in two halves was not such a risk. Not with the northern highway and its wall of pine on the far side, and the closer buildings left behind to guard the southern part of the pass, able to quickly respond to any incursions from the stair.

"Not far now," Risi said, boots clapping as he quickened his stride.

He stopped inside the nearest barracks – a largely bare series of rooms that housed a chill to the air, and distant murmurs, perhaps from a dining hall.

Risi requested their patience as he knocked and then entered a room.

Moments later, he returned, introducing Mira.

She had obviously been sleeping before Risi roused her. Her red hair was in disarray and she wore tunic and pants of grey rather than armour. But she met them without complaint, speaking from her doorway as she sipped at something from an earthen mug.

After she explained finding the corpse and only the corpse at the foot of the dam's edge on a routine patrol, Vilas asked his first question. "Did you notice any hints of pink rock on the body? Or nearby – something common to the area around the dam?"

She shook her head. "None that I recall, no. And not around these parts, either."

"And no hints of other Brutes? Nothing to suggest the purpose of the corpse?"

"No. But something happened since... a few days after. I think you should see it, Beast. We're still arguing over whether it's connected, so I'm glad you've come at last to settle things."

"Whether what is connected, Captain Mira?" Tano asked. "We have received no report."

"It hasn't been sent, in case it's nothing. But it's the trees, farther upstream. Radiant Risi can show you, as I'll be heading back to my rest now."

"Of course." Risi turned to Tano. "It is not so far. We can make the trip and return with plenty of time before nightfall."

"Lead on, then," Tano said as he nodded to Mira, who was already closing her door.

Once back in the sharp air of the mountains, the young Radiant took them across the bridge. On the far side, they skirted the treeline and riverbank alike, smooth stones of the road wonderfully maintained.

The lake sparkled far and wide beside Vilas as he followed the others, tracing the river up and through the deep green of the forest. Icy peaks capped the treeline, the Otakom Ranges just visible again, a colossal wall of stone that, if any were to tunnel through, would eventually come across the Free States and beyond in turn, Yadira's homeland.

But it did not seem likely that nearly a century ago, the Brutes would choose to leave their ancestral homes in the east so they could migrate to the barren plains and underground cities of the Free States, and then come farther and farther toward the Otakom.

Such a thing simply had not happened.

Not unless the Brutes hid themselves and their homes away from the people of the plains for scores and scores of years. *All this guesswork and nothing to show for it but a mutilated hand and a chip of pink stone.*

Once within the trees, Radiant Risi stepped from the road to follow a secondary trail – still a smooth enough path, but not nearly so wide. It led away from the Lidasch River, dipping through depressions and little rises topped by more creeping shrubs and once, Vilas even caught glimpse of a large steel beetle, its impenetrable shell gleaming.

Prized by Onathian nobility for their small but

sweet organs, it was not difficult to wish the fellow luck in remaining hidden.

"It is not far now," Risi said, once more leaving the current trail for a new path. This involved pushing through low-hanging branches and occasionally forcing their way through leathery shrubs that grew beneath the pines. Vilas pulled a leaf free as he did so, the warm scent familiar enough to give him pause. *What exactly does this remind me of?*

Radiant Risi called from ahead. "Here."

Vilas joined them in a wide clearing, where a picture of wanton destruction waited.

Most trees had their lower branches stripped of needles, broken or gnawed down to the heartwood in places. The trunks too, appeared ravaged by claws or even disease – blackened patches found within the gnaw-marks. Even the clumps of needles littered across the clearing bore traces of a blackening.

And near one edge of the clearing, a tangle of larger branches had been gathered together and these too, sat stripped and gnarled.

Radiant Risi pointed. "It continues on for some distance; there's a lot more destruction in a sort of line, but we cannot fathom it. No bear would do such a thing, nor even a roaming Bone-Wyvern from the plains, surely. Everyone thinks it is the Wahkyog, but does that even make sense?"

"Maybe, maybe not," Tano said. "Vilas?"

"Our stories describe the barren plains far to the

east and north as their ancestral homeland, that they moved across the mountains with the seasons, both this range and others. On this side and on the plains side, they *hunted* across the ranges. Nothing was mentioned about doing this to trees," he said as he gestured to the mess.

"Then it *wasn't* the Brute we found?" Radiant Risi asked.

"I wouldn't commit to that statement either." Vilas approached a trunk. Up close, the black marks carried a faintly sweet scent... spun with spice, it was certainly not sap. He reached up but paused. The darkness was clearly corrosive, considering how it had eaten into the wood – one of the five dangers.

Vilas folded his arms. If a single Brute was responsible, what was the purpose? Desperation for food? After all, the Brutes of the past had been indiscriminate in their diet – human, animal and plant, certain of the softer stones too, it did not matter. *But this?*

"I hear something," Yadira said.

Vilas turned.

From the direction of the highway came the faint tread of footfalls, of a *set* of footfalls. How many? And not following from the direction of the dam, but rather approaching the clearing from farther north.

"I will see," the Steel Maiden said, then flashed from the clearing – the movement so fast that it almost seemed inhuman. Vilas started after but she was already out of sight. The vaunted speed of the Steel

Maidens, in the flesh. *She's faster than you anyway, even in armour. Just let her scout ahead.*

He turned to the Radiants. "Be ready to loosen the Binding."

Chapter 9.

"Davorians," Yadira said when she returned, sword drawn, blue eyes concerned behind her falcon mask. "Two dozen, heading toward the dam. They should pass us unseen, unless we intercept."

Radiant Risi turned to Tano, his eyes a little wide. "What do we do?"

"We stop them, taking at least one prisoner."

"With a force that size, you'll need me," Vilas said.

Tano frowned, but he was nodding. "Lady Yadira, lead us to intercept. Radiant Risi, I take it this is your first battle?"

"It is," he replied, looking down.

"Then stay to the rear."

Either way, the 'battle' wouldn't last very long. *The only thing in doubt is whether the Davorians are connected to this mystery.*

Yadira led them from the clearing and through the trees, closing with the sound of soldiers quickly.

Between the trunks, Davorians were already visible – most attired like the woman with the Cherished Sons, with strapping or short tunics over bare chests, half-visible beneath fur coats, some also wearing black scarves. Most were blond-haired but two bore shaven heads, and all were armed with hand-axes or maces.

"Give them a chance to surrender," Tano commanded as he and Yadira burst from the treeline to spread across the road.

Vilas joined the two, his heart-rate quickening – excitement or nerves? More likely, resentment. *How long since I had to fight?*

The leader of the Davorians, a man near-to twice the size of the others, shouted over his shoulder as he charged, the long vowels of his language ringing out. But Vilas understood. *Not a single one can escape!*

Two dozen, all armed, all desperate – or perhaps professional enough – to slaughter each and everyone standing in their way, no doubt in order to keep their presence in Onath secret.

Not that it matters.

"Wait." Vilas stepped forward as Yadira lifted her blade beside him, as if poised to streak forth and attack. "Radiant, one Binding."

"We need –"

The Davorians were nearing, weapons raised. "They're not going to surrender," he said.

"Fine!" Tano swiped one pair of forefingers across the other pair.

Vilas' collar glowed yellow... and suddenly the sweet burn of the Embers lay within reach; a lingering call.

Gods, at last!

Over a decade. An entire decade since he last touched them. And now their searing power returned... yet the bitter taste of ash came too, rushing into him as warmth flooded his veins; the lightness of his limbs, every simple movement so easy now, the ache in his joints vanished, the world changing, brighter and somehow more delicate – ready to burn.

So, I am alive, after all.

Vilas exhaled as he called the Embers back home, then pointed.

Red roared.

It burst up from beneath the leader's feet and sprayed across the clearing, dark embers swallowing the man. The Davorian had no time to even scream. The Embers had already changed, a whirlwind of searing fire twisting up, powerful and bright.

And when it vanished, only a small pile of blackened ash lay atop the glowing earth.

The warriors fell back, several with cries of horror. One pointed, howling an accusation as he did – the Davonian word for 'freak'. *A familiar curse.*

But the man had no chance to utter another word, much less attack. Vilas pointed again, and the handle of the man's axe flashed white-hot. The warrior flung the weapon aside, collapsing with a squeal as he clutched at his hand.

"Surrender," Vilas shouted across the space that remained, speaking slowly, since his pronunciation of Devonas was not so complete as his understanding. "We will spare you if you reveal your purpose here."

The group hesitated, and it seemed they might relent, until one grabbed his nearest fellow. "They cannot know. Even with the freak, there's only four of them. We fight!"

And together, the men and women surged forward.

"Release another binding!" Vilas called, and even before he'd finished his words, a hail of Embers waited at his fingertips.

He cast them forth.

A massive column of fire erupted; black to red and orange to white. It shot into the sky, flinging earth, stone and burning limbs and torsos into the air as it roared. Heat blasted Vilas where he stood, but he pulled it close, absorbing as much as possible through his skin, so that his travelling companions did not suffer.

Then he cut the flame.

In the new silence, once again naught but ash and charred earth remained. Deep red and black embers smouldered where a once-peaceful section of road had stood. Pine needles smoked at the edges of the bed of embers too, a sweet scent filling the air – taking the place of words that might have been spoken.

All were quiet.

"You are a credit to your calling, Radiant Tano,"

Vilas said, glancing over his shoulder.

The man swallowed but did not respond. One hand was still raised, yellow glow lingering. Radiant Risi had stayed to the rear, it seemed, but was now stumbling back several steps. He trembled as he moved, hands hidden in his sleeves, and it seemed he could not speak either.

Only the Steel Maiden had words. "Your eyes... and your skin."

Vilas lifted both hands. Dark, near to charcoal grey now, with a trapped glow of orange beneath, where the fire ran within his veins. *Oh, I do remember this.*

The change would not last.

It was only ever apparent after a long absence of use, but even without being able to see his own eyes, he knew they would remain aglow with fire a little longer, and each time he touched the Embers from now on. Orange seeped from the corners; just as when he spoke, yet more flames would escape, only to fade into the cool mountain air.

"Y-you must bind him," Radiant Risi said, reaching for Tano. Yet the man was not close enough, and his grasping hand found only air.

Vilas faced the Radiant as the collar pulsed. Tano had already replaced the First Binding – Embers of Maelohas growing weaker, as if burning somewhere beyond the pines, and then out of reach altogether when the Second Binding snapped into place right after.

In the past, it had taken two Radiants to restore each Binding and several more in the absence of a Luminary to claw back from three.

"You're as strong as they claim, Radiant."

Tano did not seem to pay much heed to the compliment. Instead, his gaze contained a new wariness. "As are you, Beast of Khiya."

Vilas inclined his head.

"You should have spared at least one," Yadira said from where she circled the still-smouldering embers.

"My warning was clear – as was their promise."

She did not continue, just focused on her examination. Vilas faced the two Radiants. Risi remained wide-eyed, but Tano stared across the smoking ruin of broken earth to the north. "We have enough supplies to pursue this before returning to the dam immediately." Tano rubbed at his temples as he continued. "Radiant, alert Gosdan Machical that the Davorian Nation is sending troops through our northern border."

"Does this mean war?"

"Far too early to know. The Gosdan will send a messenger to the city but let him know that we are investigating further."

"Yes, Radiant." The young man set off at a jog, heading down the road toward the dam without turning back.

"Vilas, I appeal to your knowledge again. Do you see a scenario where the Brutes would willingly cooperate with the Davorians?"

"None. The Cherished Sons, on the other hand, are obviously doing so."

"Yes."

Yadira re-joined them. "We have a choice to make, don't we? The Brutes are Queen Ima's first priority, and there is still the fragment of pink stone from the hand. What if the Davorian trail leads us elsewhere? Neither of you seem to believe Devonas and the Brutes are connected."

"No," Tano admitted. "Though I still cannot say for certain either way. It simply does not make sense yet. And I hate to make decisions based on so little information."

"While the trails seem to match, there's no harm in continuing north," Yadira said.

Vilas started walking. "There is a cave system we can use to reach the lake. Have either of you travelled deep into the Otakom Mountains before?"

"Only to the dam," Tano said as the Steel Maiden shook her head.

"Then I will lead from here."

Chapter 10.

The Davorians left no trail to speak of. All the three had to follow was an empty northern highway and lengthening shadows courtesy of the dusk, light growing dull as a chill breeze slipped between pine needles. Here, farther and farther from the city and the dam, and soon from any trade route, the road was not so well-maintained, bearing shallow depressions and the occasional patch of missing stone or encroaching weed.

Even ranging into the trees or searching along narrow side trails, Vilas conceded that the Davorian warriors had been careful enough. Understandable, since they sacrificed themselves to protect their secret. *On the other hand, you're not a tracker – you could have missed a dozen signs.*

But why exactly had they come south?

Vilas exhaled as he walked. Curiosity had been awoken, and while whatever strife the Davorians might cause for Onath ought to have been welcome, put simply, it was not. The thought of someone else doing his job for him?

Not possible.

It will be me, the whole of Maelohas now, who destroys that city.

Others, Devonas or Cherished Son, no matter their nation or creed, they interfered at their own peril.

He led Tano and Yadira deeper into the shadowy mountains, and by the time they set up camp in the growing cold, still no clues had been found. They ate and then split a watch with little to share save for general theories and guesses.

And after three more nights, each growing more frigid than the last, Vilas came across the first discovery of worth – another stand of trees had been mauled. The same stripping of needles, the same discarded branches and the same dark decay left behind. Overall, the same mysteries, even if the decay seemed to scream of the Brute's blood.

To complete the scene, a lack of evidence suggesting Davorians had passed through the forest.

"I am still unable to fathom this," Tano said that night when they paused to eat from their dwindling supplies. Even supplemented by foraging and hunting, their food would not last too much longer. "If the Davorians wanted war, they would use their formidable pirate fleet – it rivals any navy. If they were planning to strike the dam, then why not simply slip through the mountains as they have, and attack it? Why go first to the Cherished Sons?"

Vilas nodded. "The same questions trouble me. We do not know who went to which location first. Or even if that woman working with the Sons is aligned with those who attacked us. In truth, we know almost nothing."

"Then we keep searching," Yadira said. "At least, for as long as we can."

Radiant Tano rose, and started to pace, spoon in hand. "You are right. In the end, any decision may be made for us, irrespective of the truth about the infiltrators, since we don't have an endless store of supplies."

"We'll reach the caves tomorrow morning, from memory," Vilas said. "If we search it and find nothing, we will turn back. It is also a less direct but alternate path to Lake Sirathemon. We should not leave without visiting it."

"Agreed," the Radiant replied.

The morning after was warm enough that even obfuscated by the usual dark canopy, the sun was enough to have Vilas sweating. The sweat cooled too fast in such brisk air, but he continued the climb without complaint. *I will not spit in the face even of such limited freedom – in the beauty of this place, chill as it is.*

They did not need to travel for much longer to reach a branching path. It slipped between three large, topless tree trunks, each one leeched of colour in death. Dark wings fluttered from a bird's nest that adorned one tree, but no sounds followed.

A narrow pass waited beyond the trunks, mountain walls rising in uneven shapes here, casting deep shadows. Old grooves had been cut into the stone, forming rigid lines that might have represented the wind.

Vilas pointed ahead. "The caves are not far."

There, multiple openings appeared in the rock-face. Some were long and jagged, others somewhat rounded. More than a few were obviously suitable for birds' nests where they stood above the others, streaked by pale droppings.

But it was the larger opening at ground level they would take and, according to his books as much as the dark cages of his memory, the opening would lead to Lake Sirathemon.

And perhaps answers.

Inside, the air was sharp against his skin, specks of dust visible where shafts of light fell from openings above. The shafts were almost golden, like lances from a celestial god, one perhaps bored enough to cast them down in order to pierce the very mountains.

Passing through each patch of light and stepping back into darkness had him blinking, but in time, larger openings appeared above. Sometimes, such sections of their path boasted small dots of green upon the walls, hardy plants clinging to the rock.

Yet the darker stretches did require the use of Tano's

glow-bone. Vilas concealed his distaste whenever the vile tool was needed. At the very least, the Radiant had the grace to return it to a pouch on his belt quickly after each use.

The glow-bone often revealed other passages, uneven fissures and openings that led away from the broader path Vilas chose, and which sometimes offered the faint echo of dripping water; hints of the true depth to the caves.

"Do we take any of these other paths?" Yadira asked. She walked with one hand on the hilt of her blade.

"No."

"Do you know how much farther?"

"There is a stair carved into the mountain up ahead," he replied. "Three more openings to your left, and we will reach it."

"When did you last walk these caves?" she asked.

"Before I was imprisoned."

"So, at least fifty years."

"Yes."

"Your memory is impressive. It must be quite the gift."

"Not always."

His memory was mostly a stinging window into emptiness; the weight of dreams that would not vanish, things which had been hollowed out and now hung within his mind… like corpses that would never rot away.

The Silk Bridge was one. *Jiana always leaned over*

it, to trail her fingertips across the water. Giggle when the goldfish scattered.

No, memory was the persistent, slicing pain from an old wound.

He continued in silence then, and similar to much of their trip so far, conversation did not come easily. Neither the Steel Maiden nor Tano seemed bothered by the lack of words, and there was no law stating that even those with but one common purpose ought to share a sense of camaraderie also.

And yet, considering both Tano and Yadira would have to be discarded, or possibly killed in order to achieve his own goal, it seemed almost... a shame? He sneered in the dark. *Listen to yourself.* Had he actually been so lonely in his gilded cage over the years, to crave the company of his enemies?

A troubling possibility.

In any event, it would not replace what had been lost.

When they at last reached and then climbed the shadowy stair, Vilas paused at its top to stare across a crescent valley, cast half in shadow from the descending sun.

Sheltered by mountain walls on all sides, the earth sloped gently down in a peaceful green from the natural entry point to the west. Grass and scattered flowers spread amongst stands of pine before coming to a halt by the water's edge – Lake Sirathemon.

The lake itself nestled into the base of surrounding

walls. Like a window to the sky, completing the illusion that clouds reflected upon its perfect blue surface could be touched. It bore a distinctive shape, too – as rather than being a crescent, it was far closer to a half moon.

"No sign of any movement, yet," Tano said from where he and the Steel Maiden stood nearby.

"I can scout this place, if you wish," Yadira replied. "It won't take me long."

He nodded and the Steel Maiden swept across the valley, moving at such speed that it seemed the grass barely stirred. *Still remarkable.* Vilas turned to Tano. "If the Brutes are here, be ready to release the Bindings. Three, immediately." He started down the rough-hewn steps leading down to the valley's floor.

"I will," Tano said after a moment's hesitation. "But if we find more Davorians, we need at least one of them alive this time."

"That will be up to them."

"We must find a way."

Vilas shrugged; the Radiant was probably right.

Chapter 11.

No Brutes roamed the picturesque valley.

Nor did they hide within the dark pine, nor even lurk beneath the calm surface of the lake where it lay still and pristine behind Vilas as he led the others toward the opposite side. There, the mountain walls streaked up toward the sky and like everything else in the valley, seemed to offer no clues.

He almost smiled. Wahkyog *beneath* the lake? *Now you're grasping at straws.*

Still, he had to examine the walls themselves, where the pink stone could be found. Even then, the only answer such examination offered was that at one point, one dead Brute may well have passed through the valley.

Nothing else.

And yet, when he stopped before the wall, success came quite swiftly. "Here," Vilas said as he gestured.

Slanted veins of pink stone zigzagged in long lines. Tanos reached out to touch the stone, but Vilas strode along further, searching for any sign of the Brutes – crushed plants or blackening of the stone, but there seemed no suggestion of deep, irregular gouges from mighty hands. The walls had suffered under centuries of wind and rain, an onslaught that left some parts smoother than others, but still, nothing useful.

"Both of you, you must see this," Yadira called, her voice fainter from a distance.

She stood significantly farther along the lake's edge, having circled around, so soft her movements that he hadn't noticed her leave, had no real sense of when she stopped following to begin with.

Vilas exchanged a glance with Tano before setting off at a jog, the Radiant close behind. Obstacles littered the shore, forcing him to detour or leap over small rock-falls and pools of clear water, sandy-rock within.

Whatever had given the Steel Maiden pause became clear before he reached her side.

A stretching row of shallow openings sat in the rock-face, each three times as tall as a man, and significantly wider too... and deep enough to comfortably hide within. Yet small piles of rubble at Yadira's feet, also following the gentle curve of the wall, suggested that whatever had rested inside had broken free.

"These are exactly what I think they are, aren't they?" Yadira asked, her voice flat.

"They seem about the right size," Vilas replied softly.

He ran his fingertips over the bolts of pink within the openings and could not suppress a shudder. *When* had the Wahkyog broken free? And exactly how many? The… enclaves ran in the scores.

How many Brutes are out there?

"You've been here before," Tano said as he waved at the openings, eyes noticeably wider now. "Why didn't you notice them?"

"The stone appeared like stone, and nothing more."

The Radiant exhaled, and it took him a moment to speak again. "So, they buried themselves within the mountain's base somehow, and slept for scores and scores of years until suddenly breaking free and swiftly disappearing? For no apparent reason?"

"None that we are aware of, obviously."

Yadira appeared less troubled than the Radiant, in fact, her gaze was a little bright – she was actually excited? "Is there anything else you can share? You know more than anyone else about the Brutes, don't you?"

"No, that would have been my mother. Or perhaps Givandal the Scholar," Vilas said. "But they were murdered by the greedy little pigs that Radiant Tano has the misfortune to descend from."

The Radiant did not answer, though his jaw was clenched.

Yadira glanced between them. "Are you claiming that Tano's forebears were directly responsible for what happened during the war?"

"While I most sincerely doubt it, I do not care either way," Vilas replied. "Since the Onathians committed genocide there are no more experts on the Brutes. The city is stuck with me instead, and I think it is time we returned to the dam. We have a lot to report." He started back around the edge of the lake.

"Not all believed in the war." Tano had raised his voice.

Vilas did not turn, nor slow his step. "That is of no comfort to the dead."

"And yet you plan to commit the same atrocity? I will stop you, Beast, I swear it!"

"Good lad," Vilas said, and his words carried no contempt, no ill-will at the Radiant's promise. "But first, we have to deal with the Brutes."

***

Returning to Otakom Dam and then reporting on their discovery at the lake took longer than Vilas had wanted – days, naturally, but if he had to go searching again, horses would be a requirement.

And his desire came from more than laziness; a new sense of impatience niggled at him.

As many as two score Brutes were out there somewhere, but where?

What was their purpose?

Did they pose a threat to the city directly? Without knowing how long since the creatures left the mountain, the Wahkyog could be anywhere. The Brutes might have turned north or any other direction as a group, or they may have split apart... so far, only bits of one had been found.

Beneath the dam.

Little about their behaviour could be explained by his own limited knowledge. *I cannot believe it would be possible to find and then stop that many Brutes. Even for me.*

And that put his freedom at risk.

His revenge.

At the least, with Radiant Risi having left the dam already to pass on news to the city, Vilas could continue his descent toward Machical's camp with a somewhat reduced sense of urgency.

But first, the Cherished Sons.

"I am wondering about Gosdan Machical," Tano said as he led them finally along the thin trail that slipped between pine trunks and toward the outcropping with its shrubs, where Vilas had first used the spyglass. "Perhaps he has found some answers in his pursuit of the other Davorian force."

"Perhaps," Vilas replied.

"Are we still planning to return to Queen Ima immediately if we find nothing here?" Yadira asked.

"We could follow the Gosdan, perhaps," Tano said. "But I do not know if..."

The Radiant trailed off, coming to a halt. The young man stared down over the shrubs and when Vilas joined him, he too, found no words.

The camp of the Cherished Sons was no more.

In its place, a massacre.

Blood spattered the walls, flung across crumpled crates and stands of weapons, across the stony earth. Everywhere. Bodies too, had been scattered, and in some places they'd been reduced to mere smears. Red, red, red everywhere; it covered the shattered barricade, pooled in gouges and puddled in the trail that led into the cavern, even streaking down the edges of every trench that had been dug.

This... is not the work of the Radiants. Not of any soldier, either.

"Give me the spyglass," Vilas said softly.

Tano complied, numb expression upon his face. Vilas raised the glass and soon found himself holding his breath. The pieces of bone, the dark intestines and hunks of limbs... In some places, orange tunics and flesh and muscle had been pulverised into a paste and smeared across the stone, as if crushed by a terrifying force.

No hint that any resistance had been mounted either – just bloodied and bent fragments of blades amongst the ruin.

Vilas slid the spyglass further up the trail to find more blood and corpses, most smashed into pieces – dented torsos, headless bodies and limbs littered between the trunks. Even the trees had not escaped the storm of death, branches shattered into kindling.

The Cherished Sons had tried to flee.

He handed the spyglass back, and Tano stared with a trembling hand. When the Radiant in turn passed the device to Yadira, her voice was soft when she finally lowered the tool. "If that is what Brutes can do, I will seek other mountains to conquer."

"Let us see what can be learnt below," Vilas said. "If anything."

Chapter 12.

Inside the cavern waited blood, faeces, and something else. Something sharp and unfathomable that combined into an assault; his eyes watered. The floor was so slick with viscera that Vilas had to place each foot carefully. As with the staging area, very few bodies remained in one piece.

Plenty of blood coated the supplies and bedding too, and clumping darkly with flour and vegetables from smashed barrels.

And not a single trace of the Brutes themselves... if it had truly been they who attacked. *No-one else seems likely.* Rubble within the cavern, focused around passages at the rear, did suggest that something large had forced its way through the turns.

Vilas left the cavern as if at some distance from everything he had witnessed, sounds muted and colours dampened. He crossed the staging area at a stride, keeping his eyes fixed on the trail below.

There, Tano sat with head in hand, surrounded by a collection of their packs.

The man's white clothing was smeared pink and red.

You're doing better than him, at least. Before Vilas drew level with Tano, a call echoed from amongst the trees.

"You should both see this."

Yadira, and her voice held concern. *Considering what we have already seen...*

Vilas looked to the Radiant, who had lifted his head now. The younger man's eyes were glazed.

"I will follow," Tano said without moving.

Vilas strode into the trees, following a path of torn earth. In places, the undergrowth seemed as though it had been mulched by mighty tools, barely green now. And from the crushed branches and gouges in the loam, it could have been a dozen or more Brutes that entered the forest in search of prey.

If that's what happened here...

Twice Vilas passed twisted bodies. They could have been clubbed by the mighty, broken branches that lay nearby, yet what slowed his steps next was not another tragedy, but a bird's nest of dark twigs and mud, pale orange eggs within.

It had been set within the lower branches of a relatively unscathed tree, a tiny glimpse of peace amongst the carnage.

"That's not what I mean."

Vilas glanced from the nest to where Yadira stood

nearby, arms folded across her breastplate. "Here."

She turned to gesture at another pile of corpses – this time both Cherished Sons *and* soldiers and white-cloaked Radiants. More than a few appeared to have been... folded before being tossed into one of several piles. Other bodies were little more than parts, and all were stained with blood or just as often, dark entrails.

Vilas knew his own eyes had widened but he did not look away.

In a tiny mercy perhaps, most of the faces were blunted or hidden. But on one corpse the face had been mutilated... flesh and muscle torn free, revealing half a skull. The dark eye-socket had become its own smaller, screaming mouth...

By whatever gods remain, why would they do this? And now he did turn away, ostensibly to check on whether Tano had followed, but part in horror. "This is a message. An extremely clear one."

"It seems the soldiers made a stand before this... display," Yadria said. "But I didn't expect Gosdan Machical's force to be caught here. They must have moved on the Cherished Sons, it's hard to say."

"Machical?"

She nodded. "I believe that was him there. Before the smaller pile."

Vilas stormed across the clearing.

He stamped to a halt at the smallest mound of bodies, and there was Machical, breastplate hammered *into* the ground.

The armour was dented so hard that blood had spurted from shredded steel; the engraving of three swords warped. Only one leg remained clearly connected to Machical's torso; the other lay in a pool of blood nearby, similar to the man's arms – both having rolled beyond dark splashes across the loam... as if the force of whatever drove the Gosdan into the ground had sent his limbs shooting off.

Including his head.

Machical's white hair held more dirt and pine needles than blood, where it rested face-down at the foot of a nearby tree.

"You filth," Vilas said softly as he approached, one hand clenched, the old wound in his side seeming to throb.

Yet the Brutes were to blame for his missed opportunity, not the general.

A rehearsed speech – diatribe, perhaps – had gone to waste now, never to be uttered to the person who needed to hear it most. He glared at the head. "I hope that a terror consumed you here, Machical. That you knew it. That your final moments were useless ones and nothing more."

"I think someone survived."

Vilas blinked as he turned. *I'm not alone.* How easy it had been to forget.

The Steel Maiden knelt, half-concealed by the edge of the largest pile, grunting as she worked to free someone – a blond-haired, bearded man dressed in the attire of a cultist, his blue and orange paint smeared with blood.

Lefios?

Vilas joined her, and reached in to lift some of the twisted, broken bodies, allowing Yadira to drag the man the rest of the way free.

"Thank..." The leader of the Cherished Sons was breathing hard, too hard to finish his sentence.

"He needs water, at the least," Vilas said.

"Right. I'll go," Yadira said, and she dashed from the clearing, dirt flicking from her boots.

Vilas crouched beside the battered cult leader, whose clothing appeared to mostly bear the blood of others. "If you survive, Lefios, I am very interested in what happened here."

"I am... well enough, considering." Again, he was not able to speak at a natural pace, but a twisted expression showed some confusion amongst the pain as he lifted his head a little. "You know me?"

"Yes. How many Brutes?"

"Six." The cult leader closed his eyes as he lay back. "I think. Most of us were out... they... attacked right after... Radiants..."

Then it had been the Brutes after all. Still, it made no sense; the Wahkyog were creatures that would defend themselves, yes, but to commit such massacres?

And yet, at what point had doubt been a sign of little more than foolish stubbornness?

None remained now.

The reason was still unclear, but the Brutes had been identified.

"Only six?"

Lefios nodded.

A troubling detail. *A mere six were responsible for the desecration of so many?* And where had the other Brutes gone? "Tell me if I have guessed correctly. They attacked from the caverns?"

A nod.

"And the Cherished Sons had no pact with the Wahkyog? Nothing to do with what was found at the dam?"

"We only used their markings," he said, swallowing hard. His gaze had drifted to the pile of corpses. "It gave them something... a way to focus the belief that we were chosen. Chosen for greater things."

Vilas frowned. "Them? Not 'us' anymore?"

Lefios laughed, a rasping sound only, as a fragile look of horror grew in his eyes. "It was all lies, of course. I wanted... I wanted to change the city. That's all. There was never... anything more to it than that. No mystical link to the past, to the Brutes."

"I see." Vilas exhaled. "You managed to flee here somehow?"

"I had already come to meet our other force," he replied, and he was blinking, struggling to focus, it seemed. "The Gosdan had already found..."

"Rest." Plenty of questions remained, and the leader

of the Cherished Sons had to survive in order to give whatever answers he could.

Vilas glanced back to the treeline. Was Yadira helping Tano? The young man had not responded well to the massacre. No surprise, considering the thorough savagery of what the Brutes had done.

And considering the trek back to the Radiant camp, assuming it still stood, starting work on a stretcher would be prudent. Then, if some of the horses at least had survived, the journey back to Onath would be more bearable.

Possibly.

Either way, it would not be a short trek. Not when he would have to carry such memories.

Chapter 13.

The streets of Onath at night were a strange blessing – not a single person they passed knew Vilas' identity, nor cared to find out. He was merely a foreign man in a dark tunic, travelling with a Radiant, a worn-looking prisoner and a Steel Maiden. In fact, Yadira drew most wary looks from people, and especially from the guard.

Eami visitors were rare in Onath, though it was not her blue-black hair or tanned skin but the falcon mask and armour that called to the guardsmen. More than a few seemed to be holding their hilts, watching with appraising eyes. Did they think they could match her?

Yadira did not even spare them a glance.

Tano was less relaxed on their path to meet Queen Ima, judging from a roving gaze and stiffness to his movements. The young man probably thought he had to watch over Vilas quite closely to ensure there was no escape attempt, no outside threats, no surprises, at all.

Unlikely that I'd bother, even if he doesn't realise it.

And while their impending meeting with the queen was enough to lend energy to Vilas' stride, even if they'd instead asked him to remain back at the Luminary Dome to continue questioning Lefios, such a thing might have been just as fruitful.

At least, once the cult-leader woke.

Voices from a nearby market reached Vilas as they walked the cobblestones, lined by poles adorned with sparkling lamps – the so-called Obedient Lights. Nearest, a woman was explaining to her child that he could not have a toy soldier, not unless it was going to put some food on the table; and not too far farther along, a drunk argued with a locked door, blinking in the lamplight.

Vilas smiled as the sounds washed over him, and while it was only a fleeting moment, it was a sincere one – for if he tried, it was almost possible to imagine Maelohas words or songs, the bustle of his old home, where similar conversations could have occurred but in a language with a more musical rhythm.

If these people knew what was in store for them, would they spend their nights differently? Perhaps in even brighter ways? After all, they had a heavy price to pay, in time.

Provided of course, the Brutes could be stopped.

From what little Lefios had shared, the creatures did not seem to be headed for the city, nor the dam. Instead, they had vanished to the west. At least, those that slaughtered the Cherished Sons.

What of all the others? Many, many others.

"There it is." Tano pointed to a three-storey building of precisely-cut stone and gleaming windows. They had been arranged to flank the main doors, climbing the entire storey. Striking, but hardly a secure building. Other windows revealed boxes of greenery, most with birds and small animals inside, some containing clear water and streaked by bright colours of restless-seeming fish.

A merchant that sold pets.

Was it not cruel to keep them on display during the night beneath such lights? Did they ever sleep?

Upon the second floor, the windows were barred – for dangerous animals, perhaps. Either way, they were no doubt all destined to become playthings for nobles. A poor future. *Could I spare them, somehow?* "You know, I didn't quite believe that she would meet us here, rather than the palace."

Tano sniffed. "With the news we bring, I had no doubts, even busy as she is at present."

"Our news must be of most concern."

"Precisely."

He shook his head. "But for such business to be conducted in this place? Is it private enough?"

"That's not for me to decide."

Yadira sighed. "Enough bickering, please. The queen will be waiting."

Inside, the large entryway boasted walls lined by feathers – brilliant blues, pale cream colours and pinks too, with darker spears also. Beads of glass or quartz caught light from the various lamps, heightening the beauty of the arrangement.

He approached a section that gave the impression of swirling movement. A lovely display – and the whole thing a work of art.

"You seem to like this," Yadira said, gesturing to the wall.

He nodded.

"But you're going to destroy it. Like the rest of the city."

"Yes, I am."

Tano called from where he stood in a larger room, one half-filled by greenery and the chatter of animals. "Quickly, you two."

Vilas joined him where an attendant was speaking. The fellow stood in a robe that trailed the slate floor, hands extended between the bars of a large cage. He was letting some manner of food fall to the waiting animal – an Onathian hound, small, narrow, and fanged. And while it munched away happily enough, tail wagging, how satisfied could it be?

"Her Majesty can be found below, with the Mistress. I'm to guide you, but if you'll permit me just a moment to finish feeding Sparrow here, I will take you to Queen Imadate."

"Below?" Vilas asked.

The attendant nodded. "That is where some of the more exotic and dangerous pets are kept."

Once the man had finished, dusting his hands and sliding a bucket away from the cage, he led them downstairs.

The basement of the pet shop was darker but offered enough lamplight to see more plants and hanging pots. And that the cages and glass displays did hold larger, more vicious and presumably venomous beasts within. An enclosure that wrapped around one wall and half the next held gleaming scales of purple visible between the stone and leaves. Vilas stared – what serpent could be so large?

"A moment, everyone."

The queen's voice. Ima was still alluring – she once again wore crimson, but instead of a gown this time, it was a silken tunic cut into a V at her neck, belted by a black sash to match her gloves. Twin golden bracelets caught the light.

Her expression was one of sorrow, something fitting for a Head of State, especially after losing a so-called 'hero' like Gosdan Machical.

Preferable to believe that her expression was merely a well-practiced one, worn for the benefit of those who had been sent to accompany and watch over her... but sadly, the ghoul had actually been beloved.

One of her minders, a heavily armed soldier, was frowning at the caged lion and the Mistress who stood beside it. The Mistress herself appeared oddly unassuming in her buttoned dress of grey, a calm and pleasant expression upon her face.

The queen's second minder, an actual Radiant Luminary, stood with arms behind his back, symbol of the torch sewn into the white coat on his chest. The same design had been inked into his sunken cheeks also.

Meveto, one of many responsible for the initial experiments. *Not that I have forgotten the hooks. Nor his expression.*

"Queen Imadate, I did hope to return to our discussion on the specifics for the State Funeral, while on this detour."

"Doubtless," she said, half her attention upon the lion and her cub.

"Therefore, Your Majesty?"

"Therefore, Meveto, I entrust those specifics to you – simply make it befitting the city's hero."

Vilas folded his arms, somehow managing not to snort.

Or spit at the word 'hero'.

The queen did not address Vilas, though she would not have missed his gesture, instead continuing with her commands. "Take Radiant Tano with you. He will lead the interrogation of this Lefios fellow. And begin preparation to travel north. While you are in the palace, Meveto, gather the various advisors. Have them wait for my return – drag them from their beds if you must."

"Of course, My Queen," he said, and as he left, the Luminary glanced at Vilas. The look was typically predatory.

They all believe they see something they can use. Vilas sneered at the man.

Tano did not seem so pleased to be leaving the queen, but he exchanged a nod with the Steel Maiden on his way out.

So, I have my minder as well.

Not that any of the one hundred Radiants in the city couldn't sense and find him all too quickly, should he try to run.

Ima smiled at Yadira. "I will have a task for you, also. I need you to keep an eye on our old friend, as I suspect they are beginning to put plans into motion."

"Of course, Your Majesty."

Vilas waited, and the queen perused the lion a moment longer, before nodding to the Mistress. "I will take the cub and her mother. I would not want to separate them."

"You are gracious, My Queen," the Mistress said, her voice soft and deep. "And I am certain they will enjoy the expansive enclosure within the palace grounds."

"I hope it so."

Vilas again found himself taking some effort to conceal his disagreement. 'Expansive enclosure' or not, it would still be a cage. And as the queen continued to examine her purchase, Vilas found himself tapping a foot. Softly... at first. "I am surprised that you conduct state business here."

She glanced over her shoulder. "Worry not, Vilas.

My cousin is also 'employed' by the Crown."

Perhaps that ought not to be a surprise. "As am I, we might say."

Ima approached. "No need for such impatience, Vilas. I am gathering my pieces, and I will send them in all directions to find the Wahkyog, among other things. You are certainly to be deployed as well."

"To the west?"

"Of course. At least, according to the message Tano sent. Do you doubt what you and he learned from the cultist so far?"

"No."

"Good. Tomorrow, you will accompany Tano and Yadira after the Brutes. That is the best path for now, but tonight I require your services for another task."

"Then, is this a renegotiation?"

"If that soothes your pride but I already have your promise."

He smiled now. *You are almost perfect, Your Majesty.* "Then consider me your servant."

Queen Ima nodded before turning back to complete the sale with her cousin, who ascended the stairs to make arrangements. Next, Ima issued instructions to her guard, sending Yadira along with him. And finally, the beautiful woman moved across the room toward the glass wall containing the enormous serpent. "Follow me, Beast."

He did so, but it was not a long walk for she stopped before a section of wall that bore no cage or case, but instead, featured three rather lush plants in pots, their leaves shiny and flowers large – red with purple stalks.

She lifted a hand, bracelet coming to her grip, then placed it against one of the plants. Yellow bindings pulsed in the plants *and* the wall. The section swung inward; the whole thing had been a false wall.

Ima stooped into the passage, beckoning for him to follow. He joined her in a clear passage of stone. Small, evenly spaced lights glowed, installed into the walls and stretching on and on until the hint of what might have been a corner. They were, it seemed, made of glow-bone, and he clenched his jaw but managed to keep his voice even. "This is useful. Does your bracelet work on all Radiant Bindings?"

"Not all, no," she replied, but did not elaborate. "Do close the door."

Her answer did not reveal whether or not it would work on his collar, either. Vilas pushed the stone closed and the yellow of the Binding blinked. "And this leads all the way to the palace?"

"It does, yes."

Vilas kept pace with her in the cool escape tunnel, their footfalls echoing faintly. "I am surprised that Luminary Meveto is not more of a nursemaid, considering what he would no doubt consider a serious risk."

She glanced across at him. "Can you not guess why?"

"Certainly he must follow your orders, and I don't

imagine you were planning to let him or any of them know that we would be… travelling alone. There must be more."

"A fair assumption." Once again, she did not offer further explanation.

"Something I need to be aware of?"

Queen Ima paused. "Perhaps. I will think upon that as we walk."

She continued on and Vilas left the queen to her quiet contemplation. It was not difficult to imagine any queen, any royal, harbouring the understandable desire to move about without being watched and controlled, but was it instead an issue of trust at play? Luminaries were high-ranking enough that they ought to have been privy to details regarding defence of the city, surely.

They walked on in the quiet, no small distance, until once more Ima bypassed Bindings via her golden bracelet. This time, it was a door that led to a dim pantry… nearly so large as an actual storeroom. "A moment and I will find some more light," she said, walking ahead.

Vilas did not follow, and not because of the poor light. There was enough for him to examine the shelves, most of which carried jars with labels for innocuous kitchen items, and though he examined each item – the bag, glass, and barrel – there was no sign of bone, powder, strips of flesh or preserved organs.

"Finished?"

Queen Ima leant against the entryway, lantern in hand.

He nodded after a moment's hesitation at what had been relief. He hadn't noticed the new light. "I have."

"Join me."

Vilas crossed the large pantry and entered an equally spacious kitchen. Its floors had been tiled in black. The same tiles climbed the walls and the long counter that ran before not one but three separate ovens.

A second light, this time a large lamp set high on the wall, provided golden illumination. It gleamed on utensils hanging from the walls in neat lines, categorised in both purpose and size.

Despite, or due to the dark colours of the room, whoever built the queen's kitchen chose a brilliant white marble for the bench-top. A striking choice, more so when she sat atop it and arranged her tunic to reveal more of her thighs than might have been proper for a member of the royal family.

Even the skin of her shoulders seemed smoother and softer in the lamplight.

"Do you wish for me to cook for you?" he asked, keeping his voice soft.

"I appreciate your attempt at humour, Beast, but I require your attention on me," she replied with a small smile. "I only have time to explain this once."

"I am listening." Once more, like her visit to draw him from his cell, anticipation had quickened his pulse.

Queen Ima gestured for him to approach as she

spoke. "There exists what we call, colloquially at least, a Shadow Radiant. Clumsy, but the contradiction in the term is apt for such turncoats."

"I am aware of them." Few in number, but able to cause significant difficulties. Once known as 'Cleavers' too, before their banishment.

But more important, he was close enough to touch her…

"Good." She reached out and pulled him near with her gloved hands, so that perfume reached him, the blend of citrus and vanilla. Her eyes were hard, and he could not look away. "You will find and kill this Shadow Radiant, Vilas. Leave no trace of his existence, not even a single speck of ash."

"You ask me to use my power then? Who will be my keeper on this task?"

Ima smiled, one eyebrow raised. "None. I will arrange for a release of a single Binding. You have until dawn to complete this task."

"A test of my loyalty?"

"Perhaps more your ability," she said. "Closer." She took his head in her gloved hands and drew him in so that his face was now aligned with her breasts. "I would not send you out into the streets without at least a taste of what I am offering, should you live up to your oath – embrace me, Maelohas."

Vilas shivered as he ran his hands up beneath her tunic. He trailed his fingertips along the bare skin of her sides and across her back as he removed the silk, then leant in to kiss first one, and then her other breast.

He let his tongue trail across her skin, circling her nipple next, gripping her back a little tighter.

She murmured her approval and he paused, exhaling softly. "You have no doubts?"

Her hands took a firm grip in his hair. "I hope you're not asking if I am scared to be alone with you now, are you, Vilas?"

This is the right moment – this will hurt, and I'll feel something *again.* He grazed her flesh with his teeth. *And more importantly, maybe she actually is strong enough, for later.*

"Are you ready, then?"

He bit a little harder.

Ima snickered as she released him, sliding one bracelet then glove free, and letting both fall to the countertop. Next, she lifted her hand slowly – more of a sensation at the edge of his vision, and cradled his neck.

A bolt of lightning split his body.

Vilas jerked back with a cry, the sound tearing itself free from his throat as he crashed into the ovens. His body trembled and chills raced amongst his veins. And though his eyes were so wide now that it caused more pain, he managed to smile.

Her deadly power did not satisfy in the way that calling the Embers did – it was a far sharper reminder of life, but it was welcome in more ways than one.

That felt… like the evidence I'm hoping for.

Ima hopped down. She closed the distance between them with a single step, this time reaching out with her gloved hand to grip him by the throat, smiling back at him. "You know the stories – all know the stories about my touch, you fool."

"Yes."

She shifted her gloved grip to rest a palm against his cheek, shaking her head. "And did you absolutely need to learn for yourself what will happen if you betray me – even upon my bed?"

Vilas nodded. "I would taste that again, if you are offering."

Now the queen sighed as she stepped back to replace her tunic. She leant against the opposite bench and stared at him a moment, her gaze unreadable. "I almost believe you, Vilas."

And so you should. "Then I will take my leave and attend to your request."

"Order."

"Yes."

"All sparring aside, I *will* destroy you if you fail to keep your word."

He nodded. "I would not have asked to share your bed if I did not already believe that about you, Your Majesty."

Chapter 14.

Vilas kept the collar of his dark coat high, sinking into the shadows between walls. All along both sides of the street so far, and within most of the Silk Quarter itself for that matter, buildings had been hidden behind walls, most at least one and a half storeys tall. Some were lined by spikes at the top while others were constructed of thick but tightly-spaced rows of steel. Most bore stone instead, but all offered only few glimpses of light beyond.

The wealthiest in the city were not welcoming.

He passed yet another small park, lit by what the Radiants liked to call Obedient Lights, but which were in truth little more than bright charms placed in saucers. Any Radiant could create them, though they were a new feature in the city, not having existed at the time of his capture.

But there was something interesting lit by the charms – large, locked boxes with glass windows.

Placed for the convenience of the residents, it seemed, the boxes contained food and wine. *To what end?* And while bindings on each box were clear, it was probably still not going to withstand an eruption of Embers.

Hmmm…

Would it be suitable to test the temporary constraints placed upon his gift?

Vilas reached up to touch the necklace he had been given; a fine addition to his existing constraints. So long as he wore the queen's emerald, he had access to the Embers. At least, enough to use them a mere three times, after which the emerald would shatter and then the First Binding would snap back into place.

Not a gift to be wasted, which meant the locked box would remain safe. And in any event, there was no need to reveal his hand – or position – too soon.

Ima still might have sent along a watcher of her own.

Her test would be more than it seemed. Even if she was trying to get a measure of his resourcefulness *and* his loyalty, even if the royal family and the Radiants had long loathed the Shadow Radiants, there was likely more to her orders.

And if truth was to be on the menu for the night, then curiosity had driven him as much as lust, as much as the need to convince the queen he was up to the task, that he would be able to earn his freedom. *Providing she actually keeps her word, knowing what I plan for her city.*

But before any such victory, the problem at hand.

A Shadow Radiant and their inversions.

To unbind.

To rend, and tear apart – flesh or stone or steel alike. Or, in some stories he'd not been able to verify, minds could be broken and cast into pieces too, leaving the victim forever unstable, their sense of self lost, bodies essentially empty…

Theoretically, a Shadow Radiant could free him from his collar.

She wants to know if I will try to bargain with them.

Whatever the limits of Shadow Radiant abilities, all would soon be revealed as the mansion decorated by its wave of galloping horses appeared ahead.

Three guards. And Bindings on the gates, no doubt.

An expensive brothel to have such measures. A sign of its exclusivity too. And yet, according to Ima, it was not so selective about who was permitted to work within; it was the customers who had to come from the 'right families'. Which at least suggested that Limatte, the so-called Shadow Radiant, was a typical noble, or at the very least connected to one.

Ima's test would also be designed to learn who was *behind* the Shadow Radiant, or at least working with them on whatever mischief was afoot. A rival or enemy? Her grandfather was the obvious suspect.

Hevolma always expected me to be close at hand. Even after the first few rounds of tests slowed all those years ago. It had always been a mixed blessing when Radiants visited less. It meant they were either making progress or frustrated by failure. The old king would not have wanted that to stop, not want to risk Vilas leaving the palace. *After all, he still needs my body to extend the life in his own.*

Even with limited results, so far.

Nevertheless, guessing without knowing the Shadow Radiant's purpose was unwise, and Ima had not been able or willing to offer much.

Luminary Meveto was another name that may or may not have been on her list.

Vilas settled into the shadows within one of the small gardens beyond the Obedient Lights, allowing himself a clear view of the brothel's entry.

"Here is good enough," someone whispered.

"Are you sure this is what you want? There's a bed just across the road, you know."

Vilas turned.

The voices were hushed, drawing near swiftly, as two figures slipped into the shadows opposite. The young man was already breathing a little hard. "No, this is better. Too many rules inside."

"Those rules are for our protection. You know that." A female voice.

"I do, but we've never done this, right?"

The slightly smaller shadow leaned closer. "Fine. What is it, Benachi?"

His dark shape seemed to be searching for something. Vilas remained still. *Best I remain unnoticed.*

There was no threat beyond drawing attention of the guards before the Shadow Radiant finished his visit to the Silken Shores and left.

"I got some sting," Benachi said, voice tight with excitement.

"What?"

"Come on, you know what it is."

"I do," she said as she stepped back, her whisper growing harsher. "And I don't want to use it; it's gross."

"But –"

"No."

"Sina –"

"Do you even know what that stuff is?"

Benachi flung both hands into the air. "Of course, I do."

"Do you? It's *people*. Actual *people*, Benachi. I'm not taking that and neither are you – it's not right."

"But they take it in there all the time!"

"Well *I* don't," Sina said, and strode from the park into the street without looking back, her pale curls bouncing. When she reached the guards, the pool of light revealed a white and red skirt and pink shawl. The guards admitted her without pause.

Benachi was muttering to himself as he neared one of the lights.

Vilas smothered a growl.

He reached for the Embers as he approached the young man, keeping his back to the street so that not even the orange glow from his eyes would give him away. Assuming his own rage wouldn't do so... yet he managed to hold back the fire and more, managed to keep his voice low. "Boy."

Benachi looked up from perhaps a belt pouch, and his eyes widened. He shrank back into the hedges, eyes wide. "Who are you?"

"Keep your voice down," he hissed. "As for your question, I am someone that will let you live, depending on your answer."

He was trembling now. "What's wrong with you? With your eyes?"

Vilas leant closer. "Answer me." Soft flames curled from his mouth as he spoke, but he swallowed them before they grew.

The lad was gaping, unable to speak.

"The most important question of your life." Vilas caught the young fool by the shoulders, letting heat pour into the lad. Sweat formed on Benachi's face, a faint gleam in the fiery light that Vilas once again worked to suppress. "Are you going to bury that sting?"

Benachi blinked.

Vilas waited. The young man was no doubt weighing up whatever he spent on the drug against the fear that his life truly was in danger. And it most certainly was.

"I-I'll do as you say. I swear it."

"Go." Vilas let the fire dim and released the young man, who scrambled off into the street.

More footsteps echoed across the cobblestones.

Vilas spun. Two of the three guards were nearing, passing through the light. "What are you doing there?" the lead fellow called, his pointed face set in a scowl. He held a hardwood cudgel in one hand as he gestured.

How to handle this, then? Perhaps a ruse. Vilas strode to the edge of the light. "I am seeking one of your clients."

The man's expression did not soften. "Why?"

"A private debt must be settled."

"I see." He lowered his weapon with a shrug. "Be that as it may, that is not something we can assist you with. Best you seek elsewhere."

Vilas reached into his purse and withdrew a silver 'tooth', only marginally smaller than a gold stalk, and one of only four from a small collection offered by the queen to aid him in his task. He flicked it across the space between them. The leader caught it with a slight lessening of his sour expression.

"There is more for each of you if you can tell me whether Limatte is inside."

The leader placed the narrow Onathian currency into his pocket. "The privacy of our clients is vital to this place." He started back toward the gate. "Be on your way, outsider."

Vilas stared after them with a chuckle. *That one takes his role seriously, at least.* The problem of entry remained, however. He left the garden and continued along the street, passing the guards without a glance. Perhaps a vantage point from elsewhere would be suitable – short of sneaking into the place.

And yet, even doing that much guaranteed little.

A name, a description and a time – an evening that Limatte would likely be visiting the brothel, a man in blue with a shaven head… it was good information gathered by Ima's spies but might not end up being enough.

Limatte might not even be the Shadow Radiant himself, might only be a step closer. Vilas sighed. *Ima could have told me, if she knew.* Most likely, that was all part of the test.

The next closest garden plot he could use would represent a stretch for his eyesight – especially if Limatte exited the brothel in the opposite direction. And more, the garden lay within view of the guards too, who would doubtless be watching him.

Vilas glanced at the walls and their barbed points. Up and over was not an option. *What about under?*

The palace was not the only place with escape tunnels. They were a common feature in Onath, after all. Especially the Silk Quarter. And few other places would have had more need for a private escape than a brothel that catered to philandering noblemen and women.

The question was, if such a shadowy tunnel existed, where precisely? To the rear of the building? Four streets across?

Time to find out.

Vilas moved swiftly along the street, circling

the brothel in a somewhat zigzagging pattern as he slipped down blackened or dimly-lit alleyways, finding nothing until he'd reached the southern side of the Silken Shores. There, a locked grate in the street with the rustle of water below… aqueduct or sewer?

The night wouldn't last forever.

He drew his belt knife and glanced up and down the quiet street – the high walls were good for privacy in more ways than one. He rested the knife's blade between the loop of the lock and raised his palm. The lock was rusted, but even so, snapping his blade was the most likely outcome.

And it wasn't just any knife… *What choice do I have?*

He lifted his hand and slammed it onto the pommel.

Both snapped.

"Damnable thing." Vilas put the pale hilt away then tossed the broken lock onto the cobbles.

The grate swung on screeching hinges, but he slipped inside and closed it without hesitation, finding himself within an aqueduct. Thankfully. Little in the way of light from the street penetrated, but he managed to avoid slipping from the walkway and into the water. Instead, he let one hand trail along cold stone as he walked toward the brothel, as best he could determine.

But he found no openings, no sealed doors and nothing helpful.

At the first intersection of tunnels, where a pillar of streetlight fell down to sparkle upon dark water, he started a circle of the block on which the brothel rested.

Vilas found himself clenching his jaw as he searched. *I'm going to be forced back above ground, aren't I?*

But light glimmered at the very next step – his necklace responded to a thin yellow line within the very wall. "Well, then." A useful secondary function to the necklace, and something that Ima might have mentioned. *Another facet to her test?*

Vilas placed both hands on the stone, sliding them several feet down from the Binding's edge, and drew the Embers near but did not release them at once. Too much force and he'd cause instability, and even a partial cave-in would still crush his skull. Too little, and he might not reach the passage beyond – a real risk, since he did not know its precise direction.

Once again, he had no choice but to act. He shook his head and let his gift free.

Embers burst forth with a muted boom. Dust and stone flew, tumbling free to splash into the water with a hiss of steam.

Done.

This time, only his second use in years, and the taste of ash was already lessening as he adjusted to his magic once more.

The Binding upon him had already snapped back down, Embers fading once more, but the necklace functioned as promised. The only question that remained was whether the emerald could count. And if so, did it consider his intimidation of Benachi earlier to be a use of the Embers?

Vilas waved at the smoke and dust as he stepped into a large opening. There, clear in the fading glow from searing stone, a second, far smaller hole. He leapt over the rubble and knelt, looking within.

Oil lamps lit a long passage.

"Perfect." Vilas took hold of the opening's edge and wrenched a piece of stone free with a grunt. A few more, and climbing through would be possible. Not comfortable, but certainly possible.

You had better still be inside, Limatte.

Chapter 15.

The passage ran free of cobwebs, or even much in the way of dust on its paved floor, for that matter. And the warm lamps he passed were full of oil too, none in danger of running out. *This route receives its share of visitors, then.*

But the fact that the path was a well-maintained one spoke as much to his chances of being discovered as it did the cowardice of the nobility.

When Vilas reached a heavy, steel-plated door and tried the handle, it was unlocked.

Certainly worried about a quick escape, aren't they?

A darkened room awaited, lit only by moonlight pouring in from wall-sized windows. The moon revealed a huge bed draped by gauze curtains and two divans with cushioned arms, these arranged before the bed, but no occupants.

Vilas crept toward the door, thick carpet swallowing his footfalls.

From the opposite wall, a shadowy figure matched his movement. He spun, calling the Embers as he did. The same orange glow met him, twin points of fire.

A third point joined the first two when he smiled.

Mirror.

His own damn reflection, in a wall-sized mirror.

Vilas chuckled as he crossed the room, picking up his pace. At the exit, he paused to press his ear against polished wood. Few sounds from beyond; a vague murmur of voices and something that might have been a pair of flutes, the music harder to discern.

Keep moving. He stepped out into a bright hallway lined with doors, the faint scent of perfume lingering in the air. Halfway to a staircase with banisters shaped in arching figures, two couples had not managed to reach their rooms. One pair watched from their doorway, as another pair of men in various states of undress kissed, locked in an embrace.

Vilas left them to it and descended one wing of the staircase, the carpet heavy.

Patrons and staff alike occupied the stair too, the workers seeming to each wear fragile bracelets of blue. A control measure? *This is not how I remember such places.* More than a few of them appeared bored, with one young woman's laugh sounding a touch brittle where she listened to a drunken noble babble.

No-one gave him much attention as his shoes clapped softly against the marble floor, passing more couples chatting, and a notable absence of aggressive clients. *Interesting.* Just what were the 'rules' the young woman in the garden spoke of? No doubt the armed guards offered some guarantee of respectable behaviour... but they were not present in the rooms, presumably.

What else was in effect at the Silken Shores – the bracelets? They were *very* thin, suggesting Bindings or some other magic?

In the centre of the room stood a wide, circular column adorned by carvings of naked figures, some dancing, or feeding one another, others simply with arms outstretched. None were engaged in any sexual acts. Nor were the people seated around the column; men and women, nobles and staff alike dressed mostly in silk tunics or robes.

Vilas strode directly to a woman at a counter where flowering plants had been arranged before a curtained entryway.

She leant forward as she smiled, revealing a little extra smooth skin of her cleavage. "Leaving already, sir?" she asked. "You are welcome to take a few moments to recover your appetite, if you wish. I can even arrange for someone to keep you company."

"A kind offer, but I had hoped to simply wait for my friend. Is that permitted?"

"Feel free to take a seat or table anywhere there is room. I will send someone to take your order, since you may grow thirsty," she added.

He nodded and headed for an unoccupied table.

It rested beneath one of the large indoor plants, this one of sprawling proportions; the Onath variety bore a faint blush of pink to its leaves, the name of which had always escaped him. It did offer both a certain amount of shadow and a clear view of the exit.

And now to wait.

Vilas leant back in the cushioned chair, resting his feet upon the table's surface. He took care not to knock over a vase of pale flowers... Supposedly an aphrodisiac. *Not that I've had occasion to test the claim.*

The night began to wear on. Doubts crept in, and Vilas shifted position often. He had already taken two glasses of the sweet wine, and spent half the time with his gaze on the stair, and the other on the door. Was Limatte even inside the building? Had he visited and left already? What if the man had chosen *not* to visit the Silken Shores at all? Been delayed for any number of reasons?

"Stranger, isn't it time you made a decision?"

A tall, dark woman approached, her expression stern but features agreeable just the same. When she stopped at his table, it was with one hand on a hip, her long green dress patterned with wreaths.

"I have decided to continue to wait for my friend."

She raised an eyebrow. "This friend seems tardy, yes?"

"Very."

"Then why not allow yourself some comfort while you wait?"

"I am comfortable here."

"I see. Then perhaps, despite your appearance, you are nervous? Or perhaps feeling somewhat... sluggish this particular night, sir. If so, you can purchase various items from our dispensary. Even something quite rare, should you wish to partake?"

He straightened. "Do not offer me the ground bones of people."

The woman blinked. "It was not my intention to offend. Yet I must inform you that even our legendary generosity..." she trailed off when he stood.

Finally, the man that could only be Limatte – considering his blue coat and shaven head – was crossing the foyer, heading for the exit.

Vilas thanked the madam and quickened his pace, following his mark out into the night. He passed the gate guards with a flash of concern, but the men were, thankfully by now, a new set of watchers. *Why not? There's not much of the night left.*

Limatte walked the streets with a brisk impatience that had him brushing by those that did not match his speed, never responding to any of the muttered objections, never stopping at any inn or tavern for a drink or even to enter a building.

Vilas trailed the Shadow Radiant from a careful distance.

Only twice did he nearly lose his target, once when a crowd of drunks stumbled from a tavern in an avalanche of limbs and fumes, and the second time when Limatte passed through a night market that still boasted performers in their bright feathers and twirling ribbons.

And when at last Limatte did stop, it was before an abandoned building located at the very edge of the city, deep within the slum-like Pens, where streets bore holes and black puddles of sludge, where the windows were smothered by boards and no whispers of music or even colour could be found.

The building was equally drab. A grey temple dedicated to some largely forgotten god. Yet despite carved proclamations that spread from the door, rising like mountain peaks, the old sign hanging above proclaimed the place to be a slaughterhouse.

Also disused, presumably.

The Shadow Radiant had already mounted the small flight of stairs, the same snap to his step, and was disappearing into the dark maw of the entryway.

Don't forget me, dark one.

Chapter 16.

Inside the old temple, Vilas found no evidence of a supposed slaughterhouse from where he waited in the darkened entryway, with only Limatte's echoing footsteps deeper within. The pale stone of the walls did not match the exterior, nor even the whole wall. Almost as if the space had been narrowed at one point.

Soft voices soon reached him.

Vilas tilted his head but could not make out any words. He crept further inside, pausing before a set of stairs and a door left ajar. From the sound of the voices, the door would lead to Limatte and whoever the man spoke with.

The stairs... a better vantage point from which to eavesdrop.

He started up and his boot crunched on grit. He froze, but it was not enough to give him away, since Limatte's voice had not stopped.

Vilas still cursed beneath his breath as he bent to

unlace his boots, carrying them as he started up again in only socks now. Thankfully, his footfalls remained soft and silent.

The second floor revealed a long balcony full of benches, half-concealed by both a rail and its low wall. Cold from the stone seeped into his feet where he crouched, and faint light wavered from beyond the rail. It was a strange mix of green and… pink?

He leant closer, keeping to the shadows… and below was not a temple hall, nor a slaughterhouse of unforgiving steel cages and grated floors, but an open space with darkened windows. Seating had been arranged on either side of a centre-aisle, which in turn permitted access to seats that rested closest to a decaying stage, where two figures stood.

A playhouse?

The odd mix of pink and green light issued from the rear wall, where more disarray was evident; heavy drapes rotted down so thin that it revealed more stone and rigid Bindings too… none of which were a bright yellow as Limatte, the Shadow Radiant, stood before them with raised arms.

After a time, the light dimmed and he lowered his hands with a grunt.

The other figure pointed at the wall. "You said you could release the Anderola, Lima. The Bindings are holding." Her voice was brimming with impatience.

Vilas frowned. Anderola? Wasn't that some sort of grave-spider, common across all the lands? Why would such a thing need to be 'released'? He narrowed his eyes. *Something terrible is going to happen here…*

Limatte folded his arms. "You arrive after a week of my work, and complain about the final moments? Ridiculous. You didn't need to supervise, Tiliana. In fact, shouldn't you be attending to your little accident beyond the city?"

"That's well in hand."

"Is it? Last I heard, Asp had to intervene. Had to send palace uniforms to your men. What happened? Did you sell them for drug money?"

"Imbecile." Her voice had grown soft. "This will be the last time I say this, Lima. Worry about your own tasks. I will deal with that particular set-up."

The man may have swallowed, may have offered a tiny shrug, it was hard to tell. But he spoke no more, instead lifting his arms again. Pink and green returned to the rear wall, and now it was clear that flickering pieces of yellow were fluttering down to the dust, falling with a sad grace that was not unlike the perishing of butterflies.

As their reputation promised, the Shadow Radiant could certainly unbind things.

He could be very useful.

And after a little longer, the last of the yellow was gone. Limatte turned to Tiliana. "See? If you had only been patient –"

Stone exploded.

Something pale flashed from the swirling dust,

spearing into Limatte's chest. Blood spurted from his mouth, gurgling following.

Vilas straightened.

The Shadow Radiant twitched upon the limb of a pale, segmented shape that crept from the hole in the wall with a chattering sound. It was the size of a horse, larger, and moved on three additional, knobbled limbs that were not unlike daggers. A twisted head swung side to side, mouth like a bowl of bone, ringed by black eyes.

It flicked one limb, and Limatte slumped to the floor.

And when the Anderola caught sight of Tiliana, she leapt for the nearest window. It scuttled after, feet scraping across the floor but a blinding light flashed.

Vilas covered his face, far too slow, but the darkness returned swiftly. He peered down again, and the creature was already crossing the seating, wood creaking beneath its weight.

Vilas ran for the stairs.

Living up to Ima's expectations meant stopping the Anderola before it left the building to start a bloody rampage within the city walls. *That's my job, spider.*

The real question was whether his gift would be enough.

He skidded into the entryway, drawing the Embers near as he did. Welcome warmth flooded into his limbs. The Anderola was already close. It twitched when it saw him, as if surprised, but its beady little eyes brightened.

The thing reared.

Embers burst upward and a roaring glow enveloped the creature.

Wild shadows of red and orange were flung across the walls, and the acrid scent of *something* dying hit him hard enough that he gave ground, coughing.

A heavy thump followed, rumbling through the floorboards to his feet. But Vilas did not stop. He heaped more embers upon the Anderola, focusing on the head, shoving them into the creature, maintaining the pressure longer, longer until he was satisfied that the flashing limbs would never move again.

The Embers winked out.

Smoke rose, the unpleasant scent now changing into something not unlike garlic. He covered his mouth and nose as he approached the corpse, warmth from his body slipping away. Orange glowed in the severed neck, and the head was no more – not even a pile of ashes remained, just traces in the soft glow. The blackened body, too, was little more than a lump now.

Good. The creature was dead and his tactic had been the right one.

Vilas looked back to the stage and the gaping hole in the wall. Just how had the creature survived, locked away for how long? And was it truly the enormous transformation of a grave-spider, or actually something similar but… far, far older?

Nothing more than guesswork.

Footsteps approached the building.

Vilas spun, Embers ready, but it was not Tiliana nor some other mysterious criminal, but Queen Ima in heavy red robes this time, flanked by two Radiants. Both wore plenty of silver rings on their hands, and while both were also generally familiar, no names came to mind.

"Exemplary work, Vilas," the queen said as she approached.

Then I was watched the whole time. An equal possibility being that Ima had always known where Limatte was headed. It should not have come as a surprise. "Then you are satisfied, Your Majesty?"

She reached out to take the necklace and its emerald in her gloved hand. "For the most part."

"Most part?"

"I did hope that we could get something more out of Limatte."

"His body is back there, somewhere." Vilas gestured beyond the creature's corpse and its faint tendrils of smoke. "Other matters took up my attention."

"Of course," she replied.

"What of Tiliana?"

Queen Ima snapped the necklace with a sharp tug, placing it somewhere within her robe, then frowned down at the Anderola. "I already sent Yadira and others to deal with Tiliana's little ploy."

Her answer was not quite one for the question he had asked. But Ima was obviously several steps ahead of Tiliana. "Then what did you learn from this, precisely, that you didn't already know?"

She smiled. "You mean, about the Shadow Radiants, and not you?"

"I do." *I imagine she learnt exactly what she needed to know about me.*

"Aside from a chance to follow Tiliana to her lair, I am hoping you have a name for me."

Not watching the entire time, then. "They mentioned someone. Asp."

She folded her arms, lips pursed slightly. "Not a familiar moniker."

"Are you expecting a link between this Asp and your grandfather's faction?"

She nodded.

When Ima did not elaborate, he shrugged. "And what of my role now?"

"It has not changed. Take some rest. Tomorrow you will be back on the trail of the Brutes. I trust you know how to ride a horse?"

"I remembered well enough before."

Queen Ima turned to the windows where starlight gleamed on several threads of white fabric. "Good. But I am expecting a lot more from you, Beast. Do not forget it."

Chapter 17.

Sleeping but a few hours in his old cell, sealed away via Radiant Bindings once more, had offered poor, shallow rest. As though tangled in webs, he'd lingered on the edge of waking the whole time, the familiar bed and pillow not enough to soothe him.

Or perhaps familiarity was the problem.

Fifty years in the one set of rooms. Even exhausted, an oppressive weight returned with the very first step inside. Nothing had changed. And why would it? There was no need to prepare the place for anything else. *They're planning to put me back inside right after I save their filthy city.*

Holding on to doubts about Ima's promise was still prudent, just as she would be doubting him despite his performance.

Nothing he saw should have been a surprise.

No, the surprise came with Tano and Yadira the next morning: cult leader Lefios stood between them, his blond hair and plaited beard clean and neat, neither they nor his skin bearing traces and smears of blood now. He still wore the colours of the Cherished Sons, but carried a walking-stick now, tipped with steel.

What had not changed, precisely, was the haunted look to his eye – gone was the religious fervour. And, according to his claims back at the massacre, there never had been.

"He might be useful," Tano explained when Vilas asked. "Or so Her Majesty informs me." Both he and Yadira appeared ready to travel, packs on their shoulders, but there were lines beneath their eyes too, a slight slump to Tano's posture. *The queen certainly has put us all to work.*

"How so?"

"It was not my place to ask Queen Ima to explain herself."

Yadira sighed. "Radiant Tano, I do believe Vilas was asking a sincere question about the task at hand rather than the queen's judgement. Or yours."

"Just so." And Vilas didn't have to lie, either. Lefios' inclusion was unusual enough, but Ima would not have arranged for the cult leader to accompany them on a whim.

"Yes, you may be right. My apologies, Vilas," Tano said.

Vilas waved a hand. "I take no offence – just tell me as we walk."

"Very well." Tano started down the dark stone of

the corridor, Yadira prodding Lefios after the Radiant. "For one, he will be of some use in the south, where there is a second, smaller chapter of the Cherished Sons."

"South? We're not picking up the trail west?"

"No. The palace received a report. A modest-sized town by the name of Pirezan is seeking help. One of the townsfolk had their entire chest crushed by something. No-one seems to know the cause."

"There *is* a chance it is a Brute, I suppose," Vilas said. He could not recall their general speed, nor the distance they might cover in a day or week or more, for that matter. "We don't know exactly where they went. Or even *when* they left the north, or what connection these southern Cherished Sons hold. I'm not sure that fully explains Lefios. What about you, then?" he asked the cultist.

"Counting my blessings, since I haven't outlived my usefulness yet."

"A fine non-answer," Vilas replied.

The man's smile was wan. "Not to me. But Queen Ima also believes I may be of use should the Davorians be there also."

Vilas straightened. "The woman with skull-earrings."

"Her name is Kivora," Lefios said. "And she was using us as much as we thought we were using her."

Tano muttered something beneath his breath.

"The Cherished Sons helped her move troops into Onitha?" Vilas asked.

Lefios only nodded, his flat expression unwavering.

"Among other things," the Radiant said as he passed a servant working to refill the lamps. The man stood on a small ladder, murmuring to himself as they passed.

They saw few others on the rest of their pre-dawn trip through the palace and eventually outside, to where a slowly-lightening sky greeted them. Clouds waited overhead, appearing to have been scraped across the sky by a rather ragged brush.

"The traitor explained a few more details, earlier," Tano said, and for some reason, it seemed he'd waited until leaving the palace to continue his explanation. "This Kivora is a *kandag* – I do not know if you have encountered them, but they are able to Leech whatever they seek from a person."

Vilas had not. While the Devonas had not shared a border, they had traded with Maelohas in his youth. Only, Vilas could not recall such a magic being common, let alone mentioned. "Leech?"

"Secrets. Motivation and life itself. Even souls," Lefios added as they entered a paved courtyard where the first few clacks of wooden training swords echoed.

Yadira turned from where she had been appraising the guards. "What is a soul?"

"We believe that…" Lefios trailed off with a sigh. "It doesn't really matter. But the soul is something intangible yet still vital. Kivora can take souls from a person, leaving behind a functioning shell, even if they become something dead inside. In a way, a servant who offers perfect compliance but who will thereafter have difficulty making their own decisions. She also claimed to be able to give purpose to corpses, though I did not witness anything like that myself."

Yadira frowned. "A serious threat then."

Lefios nodded.

"And a useful source of information, should we manage to capture her," Tano added.

"Another of the queen's directives?" Vilas asked.

"Once we are on the road, I will share more."

"Worried about unfriendly ears?" Vilas glanced around. Nearby, an innocent-seeming fellow knelt before the wall, running a whetstone across his blade. If the soldier had been sent into a random section of this particular training yard so that he could eavesdrop on Tano while leaving the grounds, then the soldier's master was *incredibly* lucky when it came to placing their spies.

There was another possibility, of course. *Whoever Tano is worried about might just have eyes and ears all throughout the palace – not a stretch for Hevolma.* And if so, just how far-reaching was the opposition to the queen? Assuming her family was the only one who would want to monitor her movements.

Or the movements of the Beast of Khiya.

Tano only quickened his step. "We have some ground to cover before nightfall."

"Can we reach Pirezan by then?" It was a well-fortified town, but specific details on maps covering the south were not chief among Vilas' memory.

"Most likely," he replied, then came to a halt. Now, Tano's expression appeared troubled, rather than revealing irritation as Vilas half-expected. The young man lowered his voice. "Let me share but one thing now, however. We will be followed."

"By who?"

"Osidani, known as the old king's Fang. I trust you have all heard of him?"

Vilas nodded, as did Lefios. The Fang – secretive and lethal, and above all, according to various wildly unlikely rumours, on his third life.

"By name only," Yadira said.

"Very well," Tano strode on, leaving the courtyard and taking them down a high archway toward the stables. "Again, I will share more of what I know once we are in the saddle."

Vilas followed with a final look behind, and no surprise, found no-one following.

But… the old king's Fang? That was an unexpected development. Ima would not have overlooked such a figure, who now, ostensibly, ought to have been working on whatever other task *she* had assigned him as Queen of Onath.

If she took the time to warn Tano, then she was aware that something new was amiss. Related to the Shadow Radiants? Or the struggle for power in other ways? There was no shortage of possibilities.

And setting the beautiful and determined Queen Ima aside, there was still every chance the Fang had an entirely different target in mind.

Chapter 18.

As promised, the walled town of Pirezan rested not so far from the capital, though Vilas still found himself keen to be out of the saddle when they arrived at sunset, swatting at angry little blood-gnats.

Pirezan waited on a steep hill, watching them with a dozen lookout towers, sturdy frames peering out over the pale stone walls.

And all manned by a significant number of guards too.

Their helms gleamed in the light – an orange that might have been painted along one side of each and every surface, including twin cypress trees that flanked the town's still-open gates.

"What do they watch for?" Yadira asked as they slowed their horses to a trot.

It was Vilas who answered. "Three generations ago, they were attacked by the now-vassal state of Barle, sneaking across from the south, seeking the nearby mines. Two-thirds of the entire town, both the buildings and its people, were lost," he said. "After the Onathian army liberated them, the survivors rebuilt with watchfulness in mind."

"You are well-versed, Vilas," she replied, eyes still scrutinising the town ahead.

"I had time to read."

"With a focus on military matters?"

"Amongst other topics, yes." One in particular that was unfinished – yet the time spent in Ima's private kitchen yielded promising results. *Such power...* But would it be enough to free him from the collar?

"We should remain watchful ourselves," Tano said from where he rode ahead. He rolled his shoulders often, glanced to his left and right at sharp sounds or swift movement.

"If we are being followed, they're keeping out of sight." Vilas looked around himself, finding only the same fields of livestock and fences beside an earthen road that led toward the gates. "And have done so the whole journey. Even when we stopped to eat and whisper."

"Of course. He is skilled."

Vilas sighed. The Radiant was not coping with the unseen threat of being followed. Admittedly, if what Tano had shared about the queen's warning was more than her prudence, then the cause for concern was real enough.

Yet her words to him had been ones of caution, not

of certainty.

The Fang *may* have been set upon their trail on behalf of her enemies. However, all she knew was that the infamous man was seen leaving one noblewoman or another's house, an ally of Ima's grandfather.

Vilas smothered a sigh. *Enough dithering. She hasn't survived all this time in the royal court without keen instincts at the very least.*

A pair of Radiants hailed them from the open gate – a young man and an older woman. Both wore welcoming smiles but neither seemed particularly interested in the specifics about the mismatched group of travellers, even if they appeared to recognise the Beast of Khiya.

Nor did either of them address Tano in regard to the possible killing at the hands of a Brute.

Instead, they requested a token payment. "Only if you are able and willing," the older woman said.

"Is this... a fee to enter the town?" Vilas asked with a frown as he dismounted, their request almost spoiling the relief he felt at being able to stretch his legs.

Tano and Yadira were already handing over money, token payments, the minor denomination only, coppers known as 'twigs' back in the city. In the past, the initials of Ima's grandfather were carved within. Now, was it hers, instead?

One of the Radiants turned to Vilas and he raised an eyebrow.

"Does it look as though I have money?"

Before either could answer, a guard in a breastplate and carrying a short spear ran up to the gate. "Radiant Tano?"

"I am he."

"Wonderful, we weren't sure you'd arrive in time."

"We sent word."

"Yes, thank you. My name is Gilid. I've been asked to take you to Radiant Quinolle. She assumed you'd want to meet at the site of the killing before we lost the light."

Tano nodded. "Please lead the way."

"Is it far?" Vilas asked.

"Only a few streets over," Gilid said, pointing west toward a tavern with twin doors and open windows. Similar to most buildings they passed while walking their mounts, it would have matched the architecture back in Onath, save for those that were circular in design or bore rounded windows. One building was even a dome with a green-tiled roof.

Another difference was clear. In Pirezan, it seemed it was common to have homes and shops adorned by flags of varying shapes, sizes, *and* colours – many with symbols and words quite unfamiliar. The old language of the original inhabitants?

Vilas did not ask. Instead, he let his gaze drift about the streets. No traces of other damage caused by the mystery Brute, not even on the street itself. Just buildings, wagons, horses and people – most of which stared as they passed.

But it did not take long to reach Radiant Quinolle, a short woman with a weary expression.

She greeted them from an alleyway where fading daylight did not penetrate far. "Here is where we found the victim, a caravan guard."

A bloodstained crack in the stones lay at her feet but there was little else of note; merely a dim alleyway that lay crammed between the town walls on one side and a stone mason...

Vilas frowned at the mason's sign. *Surely not...* "And you are certain this was no accident?"

The guard shrugged. "Radiant Ivagot witnessed something enormous and dark here. Said the sound of stone against stone was deafening."

"I do not consider her unreliable," Radiant Quinolle added.

Tano frowned. "Is she due to meet us here?"

"She is late, actually," Quinolle said, glancing back along the alley. "By a significant margin now."

"Where might she be found?" Vilas asked.

The Radiant pursed her lips. "She could be at her home. She had mentioned collecting something before joining me."

A troubling sign? Perhaps. Perhaps not.

"I will bring the carriage, Radiant," Gilid said as he set off at a run.

"Please follow," Quinolle said.

With welcome efficiency, Gilid had the carriage

ready and was soon leading everyone, now mounted once more, through the streets, choosing quicker paths, for the most part – aided by the fact that any who recognised the Radiants tended to make way.

"Much about this suggests something is amiss," Yadira said as they rode.

Vilas nodded.

"Who is most likely to have lied or misled us here?" Lefios asked. "Been deceived themselves?"

"A fine question," Tano replied. "I cannot guess, but I expect everyone to be alert to threats, no matter their source."

"Of course," Vilas said.

Their destination lay within the quiet part of town, a round home half-concealed beyond its generous garden – the mix of stone, wood, and flags awfully neat.

Save for the open door.

Vilas dismounted and followed the others into a spacious room arranged around its centre hearth.

There, an older woman slumped within a deep armchair.

Radiant Ivagot, presumably.

She was unmoving, skin tinted grey. Her robe bore no trace of blood nor any other stain. Immaculate white, but her frozen hands held a purse which clinked with coin when Vilas stepped past Quinolle, and bent to nudge it. He glanced back at the Radiant. "The sound of reliability?"

She did not respond, her eyes narrowed.

"Something else is absolutely not right here." Yadira's hand was already on the hilt of her blade as she stared out through one of the windows. Like all the others, it was rounded.

Vilas nodded. "The veracity of the initial report lies in tatters."

"Even now, we still don't know who lied to the queen or why," Tano said. He was moving around the room, searching. "Radiant Quinolle, I will need to –"

The creak of the door interrupted him.

Kivora.

The Davorian wore the same furs over the midriff-baring tunic, her small, skull-shaped earrings of bone swinging. "I am glad you joined us." Her gaze flicked to Lefios. "I am surprised that you lived." Her accent was strong, but the words clear.

"I can't say the same about you," he said as he lifted his steel-tipped cane.

Vilas glanced to Tano, his request wordless but clear – the Embers came within reach as the collar's restriction eased… heat almost gracing his fingertips, a deep warmth lurking within.

"Who are you?" Gilid demanded, the words bursting forth as Tano asked his own question regarding Kivora's purpose.

"None of that matters." She waved a hand and the echo of feet thundered toward them – as if from every direction. Vilas turned, and there, stumbling figures charged from the gardens, several rising up from the very ground itself, grass falling from their forms as they approached the many windows.

Where did they even come from?

Not a single attacker carried a weapon, and it was difficult to be sure, but all seemed to be bleeding from their mouths...

Kivora was gone.

Very much a trap, then. But who exactly was her target? No time to figure it out. He ground his teeth, pulling embers up. "Come closer, everyone," he commanded, lifting his voice over the sound of blades being drawn.

Lefios stepped beside him, but the others hesitated.

Kivora's thralls hit the walls with thuds. The glass too; they pressed against it, their eyes vacant, blood continuing to flow. It was soon smeared across the surface as the crowd grew, more bodies jamming their fellows against the building.

Scores of them, already. And acting exactly in the way Lefios described Kivora's *kandag* powers. The men and women she controlled did not attack in any coordinated sense of the word – they simply strove to reach those inside.

Creaking rose from the windows.

"They're all around us!" Tano shouted. "I can't reinforce the entire room."

"Get beside me," Vilas called again. "I'll protect you from the fire."

Now everyone joined him, enough that he'd be able

to shield them from the worst. And then he pulled the Embers closer; a sweet fire, a pressure that filled him with burning life.

One Binding released ought to be enough, depending on exactly how many were out there.

Glass shattered. A jumble of limbs and vacant faces poured into the room.

Time's up.

Embers roared up from the floorboards.

Fire and molten earth seared the room in chaotic, blackened red. The others shielded their faces as the room was destroyed. But he burned the Embers a moment longer than he might have needed before letting them recede, keeping his gift near until he could gauge the success of his blast on Kivora's minions.

When the flame and smoke cleared, a circle of death had obliterated the thralls. It left behind smouldering char and cinders, heaped around stumps of wood and stone – all that remained of the walls.

In stillness that followed, light and ashes drifting down from where the ceiling had once rested, evidence of their safety grew clear.

None of the remaining… piles of black, piles that had once been people, so much as twitched.

"Is that all of them?" Tano asked, his voice a little shaky.

"It seems so," Vilas replied.

Tano replaced the limit upon the collar, once

again forcing Vilas into the sharp but fleeting pain of withdrawal, a resultant chill of absence.

Gilid was blinking where he stood, but eventually he spoke. "Radiant Quinolle… we must report this to the Baron and the Luminary."

She nodded, glancing to Tano.

"We will seek the Devorian," the Radiant assured her, and once the two had left for their carriage, he spoke again. "Much was troubling about that. And I admit, confusing, also."

Lefios tapped his cane against the floor, ashes shaking free. "I cannot explain much more about her abilities, since I don't fully understand them."

"Something else actually troubles me," Tano said.

Vilas nodded. "The attack. It was not meant to succeed."

"How so?" Yadira asked. "The way I see events suggests the Davorian woman had gathered plenty of slaves. Gone to some trouble to draw us here with a false story. Bribing the Radiant Ivagot. It seemed planned well-enough."

"And it worked; we came running," Tano added with a frown, seemingly directed at himself.

"True enough," Vilas replied. "But I suspect that it was still a test. Of my power."

"How so? And why would Kivora do that?" the Radiant asked.

"With only stories of the genocide to rely on, she cannot know exactly what is truth and what is exaggeration about the Embers. After all, I've been locked away for a long time. This was probably a way to find out; otherwise she would have tried a *lot* harder to kill us."

"Hmmm."

Lefios' eyes were a little wide. "But why? And you say that as though such a display was nothing for you – or her."

Vilas shrugged. "That was only one Binding released."

"… I see. Well…" The man shook his head. "But I don't believe Kivora can create thralls so easily that she could afford to throw them away."

Tano strode through the char and peered into the garden, a ravaged state of churned grass and broken branches, hunks of stone and blackened wood. "We do not know if she is creating them by herself. And so, we can't assume the attack was only a probe."

"I've come to no conclusions," Vilas replied.

"Be wary that it is not your ego speaking," Tano said. "You may not be the target at all."

Vilas grinned. "Anything is possible."

Yadira sighed. "In the end, it's impossible to know for certain what her purpose was. Any guesses we make now are quite risky."

"Agreed," Tano said. "I will arrange for a message to be sent to Queen Ima, but whatever the truth, we need to find the Davorian's trail. Immediately."

Chapter 19.

But Kivora's trail was not to be found, especially once darkness fell.

Tano had eventually ordered rest for the night, finding a serviceable inn, and it was not until the next morning that a path worth following made itself clear.

And so the search for the Davorian was left to Radiant Quinolle, with Tano instead leading them westward now. They rode through endless farmlands of green and dark gold, the landscape in time giving way to plains with scattered tufts of fading grass, and thereafter, rocky trails as they climbed into the hills.

Yet one thing was constant – the path of damage and destruction.

The Brutes.

A higher priority, indeed.

The creatures hadn't always torn up stands of trees to be devoured but they did continue to dent the very earth they strode across, be it stone road, earthen trail or otherwise.

They continued to avoid towns and villages, though rumours of their passage were now easy to come across whenever the Brutes stopped for provisions or rest. Worried parents and excited children, trembling farmers or stony-faced caravan guards all mentioned a thunder passing in the night, or glimpses of hulking forms against the sunset.

But most useful were the campsites, even few in number.

Tano kicked at the earth in the third camp on the second week out from Pirezan. "This tells us nothing new, surely?" Over time, tension had steadily returned to his bearing, as if waiting for a strike from either Kivora or the Fang, yet neither came and so his frustration seemed to build on and on. "The same scratchings, same graves and piles of branches or animal bones."

"And the same remarkable map," Yadira said where she crouched before the arrangement of stone, appearing carved from the very earth.

Vilas had joined her. As noteworthy – and large – as the grave-like resting places of the Wahkyog were, the map suggested a troubling destination. *I don't know for certain.* But the varying shards of rock, constructed at two of the three campsites they had found, seemed to have shown settlements of different sizes leading in a westerly direction.

And with a particular endpoint, since the lifelike

creation of stone seemed to show the gentle mountains of Maelohas and a valley within, containing buildings arranged around a palace with a grand stair...

Khiya.

Could the arrangement actually represent the old capital?

Home.

The other stone maps had matched up with western settlements. If true now, there was still no answer as to why. What did the surviving Brutes seek? Were they simply migrating? Unlikely. Was Kivora or someone else directing them somehow?

There was one obvious goal, something that Kivora or Shadow Radiants would likely seek. The Sealed Spring. *Has it somehow recovered?* "They are looking for something in Khiya."

"A new home?" Yadira asked.

Vilas looked to Tano. "No. What everyone else sought, once they understood it. And before it was poisoned and sealed."

The Radiant narrowed his eyes. "I am not my forebears."

Yadira sighed. "Before you two break into another argument, tell me what I am missing."

Vilas met her patient gaze. "Are you aware of the true nature of certain delicacies favoured by Onathians? Or the ultimate purpose behind the invasion and wholesale slaughter of my people?"

"The invasion was in response to the assassination

of one duke or another, wasn't it?" Yadira offered. "In turn triggered by the annexation of a vassal."

"But it was a pretence. An acceptable narrative for people thirsting after a lot more than blood."

"Not all people," Tano said, folding his arms. "I have never partaken."

She looked up at the Radiant. "We have heard such things in Eami, but they are considered fanciful exaggerations… does that mean that the stories are true?"

The Radiant nodded, jaw set.

"Yes. The Maelohas have long-lived bodies, even after death," Vilas added. "The best 'cuts' are kept for the city's elite, of course. But most 'sting', 'miracle salt' and the other hidden drugs or so-called delicacies to be found in Onath are made at least in part with the bones, flesh, and organs of Maelohas."

Her expression changed from doubt to horror. "Truly, so much?"

"He's not exaggerating," Tano said. "It is the shame of the city."

Vilas frowned. "According to many, a pride of the city."

"Not I," Tano replied. "And this is beside the point. Are you saying that you believe the Brutes want the Sealed Spring for the same reason as the city fathers craved it?"

"All know that Ima's grandfather and other nobles used my people to prolong their own lives – it is the main purpose behind the tests upon me, after all," he said. "And possibly, yes. There's also a chance the Brutes are being used."

"Sealed Spring?" Yadira raised a hand. "Again, please allow me the benefit of your knowledge, gentlemen."

"The Spring of Nectar that once flowed through the capital. It fed into smaller tributaries all throughout Maelohas. It is the source of our long life," Vilas explained. "But it was poisoned and then sealed during the invasion."

"No-one has been able to uncover the source since," Tano added. "The surviving rivers and streams are all poisoned."

Yadira was nodding now. "But the Brutes might be able to dig it free."

"It seems possible."

"Or you, Vilas?"

He smiled, though it bore little joy. "So King Hevolma believed, once. But none dare risk allowing me enough power to attempt it, lest I create another, more comprehensive rockslide. Or destroy them, of course. Instead, they've been satisfied to poke and prod at me for decades, testing and seeking to unlock my secrets."

"Until now," Yadira said after a moment.

Had the Luminaries finally made a breakthrough? "Yes. It seems someone is happy for me to chase Brutes around the countryside now, despite the high value I posses."

"The queen is taking every measure to protect her people," Tano said.

"Or she has been duped into believing that she convinced her adversaries of such a necessity while they actually have their own plans for me."

"In light of your own admiration for Queen Ima, do you actually believe that?" the young Radiant asked.

"Any one of us can be deceived." He shrugged. "But no. If I am permitted to roam and carry out her tasks, I assume that is exactly what she wishes to happen."

Yadira nodded. "That is my assessment, also. She is a fearsome woman."

"Very well," Tano said as he joined them, kneeling by the map of stone now. "Then has someone hired Kivora to do all of this, or is she acting alone?"

"A fair question," Vilas said. "What of the mysterious Asp and Tiliana? Or any other Shadow Radiants?"

"One more name comes to mind," he replied with a nod. "Fang. It makes me wonder if he has been sent to protect the… investment the councillors and Luminaries have made in you."

"Charmingly phrased, but it's likely," Vilas replied.

Yadira glanced to their backtrail. "If you wish, I can scout again?"

"Thank you, but I fear it will be the same as last time," Tano said. "If the Fang or anyone else follows closely, then they are keeping well out of sight. Especially considering that you haven't been able to surprise them yet."

"Speed is not the only factor."

The Radiant rose. "We haven't solved anything here, and I think our time is better spent moving forward. It is only two more days until the border and Khiya, and the trail has not vanished."

"If we must follow them into Khiya, how dangerous is the ruin?" Yadira asked.

"Considerably," Vilas said.

"I have not gone myself, but we have records of previous searches," Tano said. "Radiants are also still dispatched to perform maintenance on the Bindings that stop poison spreading beyond the city's borders. None spend more than two or three days inside."

"Why such a limit?"

"It is not just the threat of the poison or the creatures that live within the sludge, but there are… twisted spectres in the ruin."

"As in, ghosts of the slain?"

"Yes," the Radiant replied. "At night, they lure their victims away and strip the flesh from their bones."

"Supposedly, no matter which city the fallen originally hailed from, they are all known as Anchored Spectres," Vilas added. "They are trapped, and attack in a futile attempt to take back what was stolen from Khiya – bodies."

Yadira frowned. "And how do we guard against such a threat?"

"Vilas?" Tano asked.

"If we have to enter Khiya, then I will be able to protect us."

"How?"

In spite of the reports he had read, the very same ones Tano would have been familiar with as a Radiant, most claimed luck, using clouds of the poison fumes or sheltering underground as being vital to surviving more than one night in the ruins. "Aside from what we have both read about hiding underground, I may be able to find something. I won't know until we're inside."

"Is that the best you can offer?" Tano asked.

He shrugged. "What are our options? Will you turn back and disappoint the queen?"

"Of course not."

Yadira shook her head. "It seems like we have little choice."

"Agreed," Vilas replied as he stared ahead, the problem at hand already fading somewhat, replaced by a ghostly ache in his side. *What manner of awful homecoming awaits me?*

Chapter 20.

City of Khiya, the heart of Maelohas, crumbled beneath Vilas' gaze.

More accurately, *continued* to crumble as he stared down at decaying buildings and creeping vines that clambered across nearly every surface, a pale blue that blended with the stone. He stood upon the crest of a hilltop, unable to take another step. Both hands were clenched at his sides where long grass swayed against his knees, the morning breeze cooling sweat on his face after the long trek.

Khiya, the capital.

Khiya, the ruin.

You knew this.

Being told of its destruction in the early days of imprisonment, learning that Princess Taranera had been forced to poison the spring, reading detailed Onathian accounts in the years after the genocide, imagining rubble and char, imagining the forest encroaching, rivers choking on poison, the absence of laughter and smiles of his people… none of it prepared him for the sudden hole that cut its way through his chest, a chasm that simply remained in place, cradling a new, heavier emptiness.

And all from merely looking down upon pieces that remained in the valley, the dark hints of the dying river, destruction shadowed by the mountain walls above.

What will walking the streets themselves cost?

Horses nickered from where they had been picketed, plenty of grazing nearby, but he did not turn. It was best not to take them into the city where the streets were broken, where decay and noxious fumes lingered.

Nor was it a welcoming place for people.

Few buildings remained from his youth, and those that did were stunted shadows of themselves, or half-concealed by spreading vines and shrubs of blue and faint green as the valley continued to swallow the buildings.

No more Royal Gallery, no People's Library, no Theatre of Stars.

Buildings that were not broken or fallen in a gentle crumbling had been pulled apart and scattered in halves and sometimes smaller sections that were still largely intact. Like half a window frame within a stone wall, the cut so very clean – the work of Cleavers, then, now known as Shadow Radiants.

Only, the vegetation had not reclaimed all the streets and market squares.

For every stretch of life there waited still-blackened patches and shapes, where the fires of his people had fought back, leaving behind soot and blood that would not permit anything to grow thereafter.

Or to the east, where swathes of unnatural, molten slag lay heaps of brittle white, steam bursting free to make restless columns all along the channel.

Not mere hints of the past atrocities; vivid evidence.

Of death.

So much that the numbers could hardly explain the loss.

Yet one part of the city had, on the surface at least, weathered the onslaught of both time and the Onathian barbarians.

The palace.

It stood beneath the canyon walls, the sickle-shaped valley casting long shadows. Even from a considerable distance, he could see that what remained of the place stood firm; clad in rich carnelian and mighty threads of gold that were vague sparkles.

A long stair lined by withered trees led up to the open gates, trees that ought to have stood in wild pinks, that ought to have led to the warm welcome of the attendants with their silken voices.

Inside, only ghosts and bones now, presumably.

Hopefully, answers.

"Vilas?" Yadira's voice reached him, her tone soft.

She stood a little way behind Tano, who waited farther down the gentle but blackened slopes leading to Khiya. The Radiant's white robe was stark against the surroundings, like a cry of awful pride, a symbol of those who had only murder in their hearts.

Vilas frowned. The slopes should have been covered in sweet wildflowers and winding paths of stone, places he had roamed as a boy on the cusp of manhood... *We used to rework the patterns, so the dark stones spelled out insults.* He almost smiled. *What childish fools we could be.*

In the same place, Dalia had accidently singed Jonol's feet while scaring off a bear, and he'd sulked for a week.

Unbidden, the image of his friend's broken body came to mind.

Halved by the Cleavers.

Bright blood and dark intestines spread across the road before Onath's walls, Jonol's chin splattered in blood, one hand still gripping a blade where it rested several feet away.

Fifty years gone, and the memory was still so cursed and bright.

Stop. Vilas focused on the scene before him.

Now, arrowheads, scraps of armour and even bones protruded from the frozen black slopes, where so many had died as they tried to flee Khiya. Where Machical's soldiers had funnelled the survivors into wagons, to be taken away and 'preserved' for future 'use'.

"Vilas?"

The Steel Maiden again.

He nodded to her, answering through a clenched jaw. "I am waiting for Lefios." And it was mostly a lie, since the clack of the man's cane had already drawn near.

Yet neither Yadira, Tano nor Lefios appeared to be experiencing any impatience, they merely stood and waited.

A little more tact than I expected.

"Continue," he said, and they did.

Vilas followed down the old road where stone still fended off dark weeds and creeping earth in the places it had not been seared and stained forever black, heading toward the city outskirts.

Similar destruction met Vilas there as he trailed the others – and not only from the passage of the Brutes. Malnourished shrubs were trapped between soot-like skeletons of larger trees; piles of stone or twisted steel were also plentiful. In places, rusted blades and armour.

Pieces that hadn't been melted together by the Embers of Maelohas.

The tallest thing they passed was a half-sunken wagon, its grey sides covered in more of the pale-blue vines that were returning sooner than any grass. While the others moved on with brief glances, Vilas paused to kneel before the wagon.

At its base, the earth was a mix of sandy dirt in

black and grey, with spidery lines of white spread throughout. Not a lethal poison but enough to cause plenty of harm. It was too much for grass to return; nor were the old traces of Maelohas blood, flesh, and Embers enough to restore the land above.

Instead, it was evidence of something remarkable.

A tear came to his eye.

Such soft earth spoke of two things. First being a bitter curse – left behind by a body long-since slain by invaders. He could only hope that many Onathians made the mistake of eating from whoever had died before the wagon.

From whoever had sacrificed themselves to protect others.

So, my luck is turning. For a secret could be found below such sites – something wondrous, and something that could be used as a charm against spectres that roamed within.

Vilas began to dig into the sandy earth. While the white webs would harm others, he need not fear it. After all, they were meant to guard the tragic gift that should be concealed below. *No, Vilasequ.* His grandmother's rasping tone was faint in his memory as he worked, but the words themselves had not faded. *They cannot harm you. And should you find the* eviha *below, be sure to bring it to the priests. Even a tiny piece is too precious to stay buried forever, my darling boy.*

Enough time had gone by that the *eviha* should have formed, a gift made possible only by the most precious self-sacrifice.

And there, something small with hard sides.

He pulled it free, fine grains trailing from a many-chambered piece. It bore some resemblance to honeycomb, a faint gold tint with swirls of the sun and rich earth too… it was life. Something that Onathians of the past had so deeply and terrifyingly misunderstood.

If nothing else, their inability to harvest much, let alone use the material, was a gift in and of itself.

Heavier than it seemed, the rare honeycomb-like *eviha* was too precious to waste on the pigs in Onath; the result of a life given for another's future.

What more potent gift could there be?

He pocketed the *eviha* and strode on.

Patches of blasted earth continued into the city proper, no enormous walls here – Khiya had been as naïve as it was beautiful. Perhaps now a thin beauty remained, a natural run of plants crossing and covering rubble. In places, it spanned the streets – if such a word could still be used – from broken upper storeys.

Some vines stretched eagerly, pale fronds uncurled to reveal barbs of gleaming orange. Elsewhere, they sought to strangle other plants or trees, attacking stone with equal vigour.

At times, between what could have been collapsed homes or merchants, scraps of faded cloth were visible, and even tarnished cutlery or fragments of bowls. Once, a glimmer from silver thread caught his eye beside a large crossroad and again, Vilas found himself kneeling. He reached out to lift it free – tearing the fabric.

What remained in his hand had obviously been shielded from much of the ravages of time by both rubble and white webs in the sandy earth, but for whatever reason the pile had shifted, exposing the garment – a woman's scarf. The silver thread would have once made a pattern of a flute. A musician lay buried somewhere within, her bones only.

More honeycomb could have waited below. *Digging here wouldn't be easy.*

"We should not remain still for very long," Tano said.

Vilas lifted the cloth a little closer. "Do you know what I was before the invasion?"

Tano frowned. "No."

Yadira had half-turned to keep watch on their surrounds but appeared to be listening with perhaps more patience than the Radiant. Lefios had moved a little closer, too.

"I was a poet," he said with a flat chuckle, replacing the scarf. "Something beautiful yet utterly useless."

Tano did not reply, but the Steel Maiden glanced at him. "Do you believe that?"

He gestured to the ruin as he rose, then resumed walking, this time taking the lead. He did not look back as he detoured a large depression in the crossroad; it was filled with bones and bones and more bones, all covered in the white webbing – but his jaw was clenched.

Vilas soon slowed once more, and this time because he could no longer be certain they followed a path left by the Wahkyog. "With no sign of the Brutes having chewed clear through the city, we may not reach the palace before nightfall."

"Exposing us to the Spectres," Yadira said.

Tano wore a troubled expression. "Which you will be able to drive off, won't you?"

"I believe so," Vilas replied as he strode along, not yet mentioning the honeycomb. "I should be able to fashion a ward, but we'll still need shelter. To be safe, I'll need two Bindings released at a minimum, and at all times."

"That is not something we agreed on."

"No." He waited.

"Are you planning on searing a path to the palace?"

He shrugged. "Possibly. I could manage some noteworthy distances, but I cannot simply burn everything before us for an indefinite period. There are *some* limits beyond this collar."

Tano was shaking his head. "Then why? One Binding should be enough for any surprises here. Especially between the four of us."

"No. And you are profoundly wrong in your ridiculous assessment of a place you know nothing about."

"What?"

"Queen Ima misplaced her trust in you, if you cannot

take advice from the very person she is relying upon to save her city."

The Radiant's eyes widened as he trembled. "You are mistaken."

"Then do as I require."

"I am leader here and you are to follow *my* directions," Tano said from between clenched teeth.

"By all the Gods of Eami," Yadira snapped. "If either of you want to succeed, then you had better start acting like adults. Now, follow me and shut your mouths."

The Steel Maiden charged ahead, her back straight and head held high.

Tano blinked after her before glancing at Vilas with a frown then following Yadira. A somewhat sheepish Lefios joined them, though the man was hardly at fault.

Well, that was surprising.

And Vilas found himself almost smiling as he, too, followed the woman.

Chapter 21.

The deeper they traversed the ruin, the quieter Khiya seemed – and it had not been a riot of movement and sound before. There had been no birdsong, no chattering nor even the scrabbling of claws over stone from small animals, not even wind through the leaves. That same emptiness prevailed where they walked now, still some distance from the canyon walls and the palace.

Yet one sound persisted over their footfalls.

The faint hiss of steam.

Increasingly, it was becoming necessary to detour darkened streams – sickened tendrils cutting into the earth, each borne from the Spring of Nectar. Once, when it left the mountain and palace grounds, it became the River Elorin, but now only venom flowed, now, the river had lost its name.

At one stream, Yadira stood beyond reach of the noxious fumes, pointing to the dark flow where purple bubbles occasionally burst, and shapes moved below. "I know the fumes and the stream itself is poison, but what of the moving shapes? What could live in there?"

"Onathian reports call them Drifters," Vilas said. "No-one seems to know what they are, exactly, but they cannot leave. Cannot even break the surface."

"And if we were to fall within?" she asked. "I assume the Elorin will be broader near to the palace. From above, I saw pools and small lakes in places. We'll have to navigate that, won't we?"

"The Radiants have lost four in their exploration over the years," Tano said. "Witnesses described a brief struggle only."

Somehow, Vilas kept an ungenerous comment to himself. "We need to find shelter before night falls, somewhere I can protect us."

Once darkness covered the city, new sounds would fill the ruin.

A tiny part of me is *curious.* In some writings, the Anchored Spectres were said to rise from the streams specifically. Other times, they peeled themselves free from stone or branch. In all accounts, it was claimed that their whispers lured the unsuspecting to their deaths. Sometimes, into the poison pits and streams to be swallowed up and melted down to nothing.

Perhaps into Drifters.

Yet, would the spirits take *only* those that brought the invaders to mind? *And not me?* Most likely, he'd have to use part of the honeycomb for some manner of charm. Not precisely what grandmother or the priests would have had in mind, either – but she did not envision such a future. *None of us did.*

The day continued to wear on, and their trek became more of a search, but with little luck.

Even in the homes or buildings that stood half-intact, some held together by the vines, little shelter could be found. Nor much of use. Scraps of rotting timber, thin and grey, kitchens empty of utensils, and as with most other parts of the city, few hints of skeletons either – at least, no Maelohas. *Harvested, one and all.*

Even Onathian soldiers were rare, their armour providing the answer as to why their bodies had been left behind by scavengers and other scum of Onath.

Only once did Vilas find another stretch of white web worth searching, but no more *eviha*.

"What about that one?" Tano eventually pointed toward a three-storey building to the east. Like most that remained standing, its sides were covered in twisting plant-life, but here was a small miracle – Soft Fairysbreath had survived. It bore some resemblance to dandelion clocks in pink and yellow, but up close, its shape was more triangular.

The delicate plant had once filled the Northern Groves, where in the summer months, the palace would host parties for the various artists of the city, always aglow with smiling faces.

And there, in the groves that no longer existed, where the Silk Bridge once stood, Jiana would live forever. If he left the others behind and went there, would he hear the faint scratching of her quill as it slipped across the pages?

Vilas hesitated. *Jiana.* Deep inside, he had never promised her sweet memory revenge, never promised her that Onath would be punished – never done anything of the sort.

The last thing she would have wanted was more suffering.

He swallowed. *Forgive me, Ji, but I do.*

"Well?"

"Yes." Vilas turned back to the Radiant. "We might get lucky, at last."

Yet while the weed-choked streets led them quickly to the tall building, one that was once quite an opulent inn at a glance, another stream of poisoned-sludge barred their way. Fumes rose from the surface, ever-shifting and flowing. The stream spread around the building like a forked tongue and, combined with the setting sun, presented a serious impediment.

"Can you... I don't know. Ease the suffering here?" Lefios asked, his eyes appearing quite tired. And though he leant on his cane, he was still upright. Perhaps his other wounds were sapping his strength.

An elegantly phrased request, but even if Vilas knew how, was it even something the spectres would accept? None had appeared yet. Even so, it was apparently impossible to predict which parts of the ruin they would emerge from on any given night.

Whatever the result, they had to be taken into

consideration, like any other obstacle.

Vilas shrugged. "If you've noticed that I've stopped a few times to dig, then you'll be pleased to know that I do possess what I need to try, once we are actually inside."

"That's a comfort."

Tano was pacing before the stream, keeping out of reach of the poisonous steam.

The width of the barrier was too great to simply leap across, not to mention the mist, which would likely kill everyone if too much was inhaled. *And damage me, even if I don't know how much.* But with some sort of makeshift bridge, they'd reach shelter before darkness.

In addition to the threat of the Drifters, the sludge itself could eventually melt through even stone, but again, it was the wisps of steam that posed the more immediate threat – clinging to any who drew too close and in time, withering their flesh.

Something such early Onathian raiders, desperate to return to the city for one last corpse, had discovered for themselves.

"It does look less damaged than other buildings." Yadira pointed. "A few windows holding glass there, too. Can we find a way?"

Vilas nodded. On the ground floor, there was even a door of steel still on its hinges, somewhat frail-looking, and ajar, but in one piece.

"We have to build a bridge," Tano said with a small sigh.

Lefios nodded. "Using what?"

"Stone. I will bind it."

Lefios glanced around at the vine-choked rubble, thumb tapping upon his cane. "I doubt we could heave enough large stone into the stream for a series of stepping stones. Can you make a ledge? We could leap from that point."

Yadira glanced up at the slowly setting sun. "I think we could manage if we get a head start."

"Then let's use the last of this light," Vilas said as he moved to the nearest pile of tumbled stone half-concealed by undergrowth. Calling the Embers forth, courtesy of the single Binding that had been released, he let flame blossom and sear away the vines, leaving only a few smouldering scraps when he cut the fire.

Then, he lifted a hunk of stone free – heavy but not impossible to carry.

Yadira and Tano joined him, Lefios offering an apology, and together they heaped stone at the stream's edge. They did their best to arrange it in a large square, and while the pieces were not uniform at all, the Binding would be up to the Radiant. Vilas quickened his step between trips as the sky dimmed.

He was sweating by the time they'd gathered enough material, but the light had not quite vanished when Tano finally knelt before the collection and closed his eyes. He raised both hands and the faint yellow lines appeared.

Stone shifted closer, clicking together as the

Bindings brightened, threading through in sharp angles. And while it was by no means a seamless raft that now lay before Vilas, the makeshift ledge would be good enough – especially when Tano moved his hands together and rested one over the other, as if to mimic a base and ledge.

The 'raft' trembled as its Bindings flared. The stones ground together, folding into a shape that matched Tano's movement until it sat perched on the edge of the poison stream, both elevated and extending out over the flow.

But the Radiant had not finished.

Next, he rested both palms on the ground. Bindings shot down into the earth. Tano remained in place, eyes still closed, before finally lifting his hands with a long sigh. He did not immediately climb to his feet either.

"I have never seen a Binding *created* before. Is it complete?" Yadira asked, a trace of wonder in her voice.

Tano nodded. "I'll need a moment."

Yadira moved to his pack and pulled a flask free, handing him the water. The Radiant drank, taking deep breaths between mouthfuls.

"I didn't realise it was so exhaustive," she said.

He gestured to the stone ledge. "That sort of Binding is quite irregular. Most of what we do is reinforce or create simpler Bindings. This was like... lifting the entire structure."

"Is that how the Luminary Domes were built?"

"It was. But it took many, many Radiants to complete

that feat. Two-score of those tasked with constructing it did not actually survive."

"Oh."

Lefios was examining the ledge. "It is impressive that you were able to do this alone – no wonder they call you strongest."

Tano shook his head. "It is the strength of my Bindings that most find noteworthy. Any single Radiant could do what I have done here."

"Will yours then last longer?" Lefios asked. "Be harder for Shadow Radiants to break, for example?"

"Essentially."

An interesting little detail. Vilas smiled. "Thank you, Tano. Let us know when you are ready."

The Radiant rose with a nod. "I am fine now."

Vilas moved to the ledge, climbing easily. The fumes stung his eyes as he gauged the distance – quite easy, now that the Binding was in place. No tendrils of mist from below, and only hints of the Drifters in the growing dark.

Hurry it up.

He backed up, then took a running leap.

Air flowed across his face – and then he hit the stone, landing on the far side easily.

There, Vilas called more Embers forth, letting them simmer just beneath the earth nearby, casting a warm glow and providing extra light for everyone else.

Yadira followed, lithe and graceful, with Tano next and then only Lefios was to leap.

The man winced as he climbed, his cane clicking against the uneven stone.

"Oh, we are fools," Yadira said. "Your injuries… Can you make the leap?"

"Yes, but I suspect my knee will buckle."

The Steel Maiden stepped closer. "I am ready."

He thanked her and lifted his cane. "And these." He tossed the cane first, which Yadira caught and handed to Tano. Next came the man's pack, and then he started his own run up, before pushing off from his stronger leg.

Lefios landed with a thud and a grunt – and as predicted, his legs buckled.

Yadira caught him.

"Thank you all," he said, and there was a slight catch to his voice.

Pain? There was a chance it could have been embarrassment, by the way Lefios busied himself with readjusting his pack.

Tano handed the cane back with a nod. "Let's search for a suitable room."

Inside the inn, as confirmed by a large reception area and adjoining tavern both cloaked in shadow, dust ruled over old stone and encroaching vines. Their barbs gleamed in the flickering torchlight as Yadira raised a burning brand. The vines had not stopped with the walls, managing to enshrine a mirror too, allowing only small slices of light to be reflected.

Despite the upper storeys bearing just as many holes

and gaps in both ceiling and floor, once they trudged back downstairs and searched for a cellar, they were blessed with success… for the most part.

Damp and dark, and bearing its share of rotting lumps that seemed little more than mould, the space would have to do.

Vilas set to work burning the worst of the mould, white-hot Embers reducing the amount of harmful smoke produced as Tano and Lefios started on a campfire.

When the room had cleared for the most part, Yadira worked under Vilas' direction to affix a spare blanket to the entryway, concealing the steps. "It's not perfect," she said.

"Better than nothing," he replied, and motioned for her to join him with the others, where bubbles chattered away in the pot. "I have only witnessed this once, as a child, so while I am confident in the result, the specifics are lost to me. The priests and priestesses of Khiya banished all manner of illnesses, both of the body and the mind – some of them fatal – with something that can be translated into the Golden Haze of the Sun, which is in turn something that comes from the *eviha* I have."

"How do we create this haze?" Tano asked.

Vilas withdrew a piece of precious *eviha* and broke off a large section, brushing at a few final grains of sand. "We burn this."

"Assuming it works, how long will it protect us?"

Vilas stared into the *eviha*'s chambers, where the comb darkened, though no answers lay within. "I do not know. My estimate is this night only."

He frowned. "And if it doesn't?"

"Whoever is on watch must rouse the rest of us if there is a threat. Then we flee."

"So be it," Tano said.

Vilas broke the *eviha* in half again, and placed it upon the flames, which at first did not seem to have much effect.

"Will it change the flavour of our meal?" Lefios asked.

"Yes. It will taste better. Another benefit, which will come from the room as much as the food itself, is that any wounds we carry will improve by morning."

"Amazing," the younger man replied, one hand drifting to his knee.

Thin wisps of golden, shimmering smoke rose from the fire, and with it, a welcome aroma that seemed to prevent any further conversation.

Vilas could not fathom the scent; it lay somewhere between cinnamon, vanilla, and the stark beauty of pine needles. It brought with it a vast sense of warmth that was not related to heat at all, but that of comfort.

An invisible tightness to his shoulders eased, and he took a deep breath, not the only one to do so, as the others already wore relaxed smiles. "This is… unbelievably wondrous," Tano said softly.

"So it is," Vilas replied with a smile of his own, though it was not possible to do so without regret. *Who gave their life to protect another, so that we can now enjoy life?*

And would that brave person have wanted to share such a gift with an enemy?

Were they less like me and more like Jiana? A sweet child who would not, for even a single moment, have wanted it any other way?

"Do we simply add another piece of the *eviha* when it is our turn to watch?" Yadira asked.

Vilas nodded. "That is all." A haze of soft gold was filling the room, and it continued to linger, as if possessed of a benevolent weight.

Even during their stew of pork and vegetables, and afterwards, as he sat awake and listened for threats, the gold remained in place, fed by more smoke, and not even a moment of discomfort.

If anything, breathing it in only brought more relief.

Once, Lefios stirred. His face no longer bore signs of the pain he'd been concealing, and though he woke, and soon rose to offer a turn at watch, Vilas only waved the younger man back to rest.

"Do not worry. I am watching."

And so the night passed, and never did Vilas grow weary.

Not weary, but once curious. Just enough to slip through the curtain and climb the stair – and he'd barely taken more than a handful of steps when the first whisper reached him.

Join us.

Innocuous enough…

But the voice was soon joined by another, and a third and fourth and on until there seemed to be dozens of them. More. All calling his name, urging him to leave the edge of safety, to leave the basement, leave the inn and see who they wanted him to meet.

Come quickly, she is waiting.

And with those words alone, Vilas had heard enough. He backed down the steps as the chorus of whispers began to hiss and crackle.

Your sister is waiting.

Vilas flinched, but he was already through the curtain, and then a beautiful, golden haze muffled the voices.

Chapter 22.

Having survived the night, and using all but a tiny wedge of the *eviha* to do so, Vilas led the others at a brisk pace through the sun-dappled ruins, ducking under barbed vines and detouring steaming pits and rivulets of poison alike.

The threat of a second night in the city soured his morning.

Despite not having slept, not a single bone in his body felt any heavier than a feather, no muscles complained and every movement was easy. His mind was clear – a dream of convenience. The *eviha*'s haze was a blessing that could well last for days, for all he knew.

And yet, simmering anger lingered.

At first, it was the lie told by the Anchored Spectres. *She was* not *there.*

But before too long, the realisation that every memory was being replaced by yet another image of ruin started to weigh more heavily, topped with nagging confusion as he strode toward the palace, slowly growing nearer.

Where were the Brutes?

If they had approached the palace from another point of the ruin, what did that mean? Who – or what – would be waiting for them?

Why did their trail of destruction vanish? *Is it yet another hidden skill of the Davorian?*

"There's something moving up ahead," Lefios announced. He still walked with his cane, but his movements appeared smoother. Even Tano was no longer glancing along their back-trail for signs of followers, a habit he'd been unable to break until this point.

Tall figures moved amongst the trees, pausing once they entered the cluttered street. Vilas straightened at their odd but familiar form. While their legs appeared almost spindly, the limbs were wiry and deceptively strong. They had to be to support the heavier torsos and their four arms. Even their long, almost mournful faces probably added to the weight.

Not that the creatures were stone-like Brutes by any stretch. Instead, they were covered in grey fur, save for part of their torsos and palms, and rings around narrow eyes… eyes that rested low upon each side of their faces.

Up close, quite disconcerting, especially for a boy not expecting to encounter them in the hills. *That was a* long *time ago.*

"What are they?" Yadira was yet to draw her weapon, but she did have a hand on the hilt of her blade.

"Nopariv. They are gentle," Vilas replied.

The Nopariv approached, crossing the stones steadily. As they moved, makeshift bandages became clear on two of the creatures – what seemed to be a mix of leaves, mud and rags covering one forearm and for another of them, the ankle.

"What do they want?" Lefios asked, and his expression was tinged by wonder, it seemed.

"I do not know. They lived in the mountains above, and cannot speak," Vilas said.

Patches of a purple taint were visible on their fur when creatures stopped and then conferred – at least, they stood with heads close together. *Poisoned by the genocide.* From such a short distance, the scent of musk was strong.

Time passed, and still the Nopariv remained together, heads making small movements, long-fingered hands occasionally rising and pointing. *At us.* But not always, since the creatures sometimes pointed toward the palace.

"And you are certain they won't attack?" Tano asked.

"Unlike the Onathians, they have never attacked my, or any, people."

The Radiant sighed but seemed satisfied with Vilas' answer.

"Do we continue on, then?" Yadira asked.

"A moment longer, if you will," Vilas replied. It

seemed one of the Nopariv carried a rather large bag. This, too, had been fashioned from castaway or forgotten items. Together, they opened the bag and sifted through a moment. One soon lifted something free, hidden in its large hand.

It looked to Vilas then, clearly meeting his gaze, and raised one of its other hands to beckon him closer.

This is unusual. He stepped forward.

"Are you sure it's safe?" Lefios asked.

"I am certain." Vilas extended his arm, and the Nopariv opened its hand. Two items sat in its palm.

A tarnished key, the royal fire-lily carved upon the bow, and a small coin – tiny numbers and an image of old King Fiious both quite faint. Fiious, who had commissioned Vilas' first official work for the court...

Tears softened his vision, and he looked back up at the Nopariv. "You want me to have these?" he asked, speaking in Maelohas. And though it had been a long time since he'd spoken such words to any but himself, they came easily.

One of its other hands closed his own over the coin and the key. And then the Nopariv turned away, starting back along the street, the others following.

"Wait. What about your wounds?" he asked.

But the Nopariv did not turn, continuing back into the trees at a steady pace, this time following the lay of the land downhill.

Vilas returned to the others, revealing the key only. "It may grant access the royal chambers, or the Sanctum, possibly even the Spring itself."

"Assuming the Brutes haven't smashed their way within."

"Yes."

"Then… they recognised you." Yadira stared after the Nopariv, her expression closer to Lefios' now.

"Somehow."

"And you spoke to them," Tano said.

"I asked if the key was for me, but I don't know if they truly understood." How did the Nopariv recognise him? Fifty years without them seeing another Maelohas. And they had not been so old, either, judging from the colour of their fur, which would turn white as the decades wore on.

Nopariv sightings in the surrounding mountains had always been rare. Even in his grandmother's time, stories were few about human and Nopariv encounters. *Let alone such interactions.*

Vilas continued on, heading for the broken thoroughfare that would take them to the palace. "We cannot spoil this fortune. Let's not slow down."

Chapter 23.

Poison flowed from the dark of the mountain range. Cursed streams encircled and cut through palace walls and buildings alike, twisting through the stone and marble to spread into a diseased maze below.

It was not only rubble and liquid-venom that obstructed access to the palace – something grew from death. Fumes obscured the finer details, but Vilas saw enough from where he stood on the fourth storey roof of a nobleman's manor.

A range of unnatural plant-life ringed the palace. Varied in size, shape, and state of pestilence, it was no small obstacle.

Does it also protect some final secret to be found in the palace? After all, poisoning the Spring of Nectar had been an act of defiance as much as defence. Now, decades later, few were welcome in the palace.

As if the entire ruin had grown and changed into a living, toxic barrier.

But in order to protect what, precisely? Hallowed ground?

Or the unlikely restoration of the Spring?

He leant against the empty window frame, rotten wood cold. The plants twitched as they drank from the poison streams below, in some mockery of life. Where the green of leaf or bough turned a blackened purple, bulbs of pink had also grown, appearing as spheres of stretched skin... and even as Vilas attempted to plot a path toward the grand stair with his gaze, two of the bulbs splattered beneath the high sun.

A shame those plants couldn't have been there to ruin the lives of the Onathians all those years ago.

Vilas spat, then pushed himself from the window.

The easiest path to the palace would be if Tano released the second Binding. Just a simple matter to melt whatever stood before them, let the Embers burn straight and *deep*. Then, when everything cooled, the furrow of melted stone would create a way clear of threats, like an empty riverbed.

Possibly.

Of course, the others were searching too, but even if one of them found something easier...

I want to destroy something.

Even clearing such blemishes on the land would do.

Whatever calming effects the Golden Haze had offered were now long-gone. Deep within, rage lay coiled around another emotion – strangling it, near enough to death that it could make no sound. Still, it was there. Fear. What new, relentless horrors would he find within the palace itself?

Things that even the history books had omitted.

I cannot see her room.

"Vilas."

Yadira stood in the doorway, pale eyes difficult to read behind her half-mask. Her winged breastplate of silver bore marks and scuffs now.

"Yes?"

"It's time to rejoin Tano and Lefios." She looked to the window. "The cellar offered no hidden passage that I could find, just like the other buildings. Any ideas up here?"

"One," he said, and explained.

"I admit that would be impressive, if it worked." She paused. "Vilas, will you admit something?"

Curious. "Admit?"

"I will ask you now, in case you wished to keep your answer from Radiant Tano," she said, her voice as calm – and kind – as ever. At least, as calm and kind as when she was not exasperated with them.

"Am I so fragile-seeming?"

She shrugged. "Say… rather, quick to anger and ill-willing to appear vulnerable before others."

Vilas burst into laughter. "That is cutting, My Lady." And all the more so because it was probably at least partially accurate. "Please, ask your question."

"Very well. Will you tell me, back with the Nopariv,

did you ask about their wounds?"

He raised an eyebrow. "That is not what I expected."

"Is that your answer?"

"No," he replied. He started walking for the exit. "I asked."

"Even though they could not understand?"

He stopped before her. "Are you accusing me of lying about their ability to speak? Is that what this is about?"

Yadira sighed. "And you prove my words. No, Beast. That is not what I am doing. I simply wanted to learn more about *you*, the person."

"I see." He hesitated; how neatly she had cut through his distrust. "It was instinct – they need not have suffered."

"Thank you," she said, and the woman seemed pleased.

"Very well." He started down the staircase.

At the bottom, they waited on the ground floor, watching through the empty windows for Tano and Lefios to approach. And when the man in white first appeared, cult-leader in tow, the pair detoured twisted steel left from the frame of a nearby carriage, moving with a purposeful stride.

"What have you found?" Vilas asked as he left the building to meet them.

"The entry point for the Brutes," Tano said, a frown upon his face. "It's not far."

Finally. "Lead on."

Tano circled back the way he'd come, threading through and over thin streams of the poison, sometimes over makeshift bridges – one of which he mentioned having to construct by himself. But when the Radiant stopped before a far larger bridge of stone, he pointed. "This one, I did not create."

Melted remnants belonging to the original bridge still spanned one of the broader sections of what had once been River Elorin, once fed by the clear and beautiful Spring of Nectar. Other stone and sometimes dirt, branches and diseased plant-life had all been smashed together to restore the bridge, Binding a new walkway to span the flow of sludge.

Bindings, of course, meant Radiants.

Shadow or Luminary?

A faint haze followed the river. Whenever a bubble burst, or something that could have been a Drifter stirred beneath, creating ripples, the colours were purple and pink with touches of greasy yellow.

Perhaps worst of all, a sweet scent filled the air.

"Based on freshly turned stone and earth, it's obvious the Brutes helped tear up the materials," Lefios said. He made a sort of looping gesture toward the bridge's mid-point, his expression somewhat flat. "There's more, on the other side."

Vilas strode around to find a section of bridge that did not match the materials used elsewhere, a section with plenty of orange and blue fabric… and blood.

Someone had taken several – or at least one of the

cultists, and used them to complete the bridge.

Beyond the exceptional but perhaps unsurprising cruelty of those that had gone before, there was a new concern. "I see Kivora is either working with or directing not only the Brutes, but a Shadow Radiant," Vilas said. "And possibly a Luminary, too. Any ideas, Tano?"

"Several. You may even know some of the names: Tiliana and her probable master, Asp, come to mind first. If I'm right, it also doesn't mean they are alone in this."

One name the young Radiant had left out was Meveto. *Is that possible? Or just my distaste for the Luminary?* Meveto and the king had worked hand-in-glove for decades, why not now, to interfere with Ima's plans?

To take the Spring for themselves – if it really had been cleansed, somehow. *Which I cannot believe happened by some accident of time.*

"Should figuring out exactly what they want help us discover who they are?" Lefios asked.

Tano spread his hands. "Possibly."

"Don't we know already?" Yadira asked. "The Sealed Spring, yes?"

Tano nodded. "Yes, but I think the specifics of *afterwards* could help. Meaning, once they unseal the spring, what then? If she's here, will Kivora try to keep it for herself? Does she send its water back to Devonas? And what has she promised the Brutes?

Radiant involvement suggests the power struggle in the capital to me, but how will having access to the Spring aid that struggle exactly, and aid whom?"

"Competing interests suggest eventual betrayal," Yadira added.

Tano paced, keeping clear of nearby fumes. "There are also several nobles connected to the Fang. They might be seeking the Spring independent to Kivora. If so, I believe they would use the water for themselves to create an endless dynasty, and trade in Spring water thereafter."

"I cannot imagine such people sharing," Yadira said.

"Nor I, and it is exactly the sort of outcome Queen Ima would want stopped."

"I believe we are all forgetting one thing," Vilas said. "There is no guarantee that the Spring can be accessed. Nor that it is even safe, if so. This could all be for nothing, on everyone's part."

"We must stop the Brutes and uncover the details of the conspiracy," Tano said.

"I suppose you do, at that."

Tano did not respond to Vilas making the distinction. And usually the Radiant would have done so. Was he purposefully ignoring any attempt at antagonising, or was it preoccupation?

Aided by his cane, Lefios took a few steps away from the river as a wave of fumes shifted on the wind. "Then can we assume that Kivora or this Asp or the nobles behind the Fang actually have something up their sleeve? Other than the Brutes, in one case. That once they uncover the Spring, they believe they can restore it, should it need as much?"

"*That* is a concern," Vilas said. "It may be possible, but I do not know. One thing I believe is exceedingly obvious, especially having come here, is that the Spring of Nectar will absolutely need to be cleansed."

"They *have* been experimenting on you for decades," Tano added, nodding slowly. "They may have an answer, after all."

"Vilas, is there truly nothing else you can offer, before we head inside?" Yadira asked. She was honing the edge of a long dagger. "You lived here, after all."

"Even in a society that valued poets, I was hardly privy to the inner workings of the palace, let alone the Sacred Spring itself."

"Then what did your role entail?" she asked. "Because the most powerful warrior in all of Maelohas' history does not strike me as synonymous with poet."

"Hmmm. You seem full of insults today."

She raised a hand. "Please. That was not my intention."

Vilas shrugged as he started across the bridge, not bothering to see if they followed.

Time to confront the palace.

Chapter 24.

Light cut into the palace interior as he searched alone, spearing through holes in the ceiling and roof, sometimes gaping like wounds, sometimes creating narrow beams, and overall, equally effective as the surviving windows.

Together, they lit up yet another vast dearth of life, creating suggestions in the shadows as clearly as they illuminated dust-covered floors and gardens, or the generous alcoves that housed shattered sculptures and frames, or the piles of leaves caught between melted columns of stone and steel.

Everywhere he turned.

Everywhere, the absence pummelled at his mind.

The beautiful statue of entwined swans at the foot of the grand stair, their feathers so present that one could have fallen free at any moment...

Instead, nothing remained.

And to the left, where the revolving rooms led

out to the Visitor's Garden, a painting of three deer arranged before a sunset of orange and blushing pink, their silhouettes strong and reliable…

Gone.

Not a single scrap of canvas left, no frame, no hint of the masterwork; the piece he had tried to reach out and touch as a child, the weight of the brushstrokes in paint simply mesmerising.

Gone.

There was no escape from the pain.

In every room, every hall, everything beautiful or meaningful, anything whatsoever that a person had created was now long-vanished or destroyed. As though, for the Onathians, it wasn't enough to slaughter, capture, or drive the people out, to *harvest* them, but all traces of what they made had to be destroyed too.

Even carven words that rested above a hearth in one of the royal rooms no longer whispered to him when he stood before them with a glare. The oldest Maelohas ballad, almost a benediction for welcoming a loved one home. Only the opening verse had been used in the carving — yet even those three lines had been chipped away.

And in its place, a tally.

Of Maelohas killed. Signed. *Signed.*

"I will find your descendants," he said from behind clenched teeth.

Footsteps approached — only one set, but a regular

tapping to go with it, and when Vilas turned, he found Lefios, relief upon the man's face. "I'm glad I found you."

It took them some time to come seeking him. "Trouble?"

"When you slipped away, we weren't sure what had happened."

Vilas waited.

Lefios leant against the doorframe with a sigh. "There's no way through the halls. We'll need to go through the Greenhouse, like you feared."

"And Tano needs me to burn the toxic plants."

"We all do."

Vilas nodded, striding from the room. *A wish for violence granted, at last.*

Back in the central halls, his boots clapped against the floor – a floor that was, once again, suspiciously free of evidence that the Wahkyog had passed. Other options existed, but who knew the city so well to lead them?

There was another stair leading up to the throne and ballroom, this one more… whimsical, with its quartz colours, delicate pinks and yellows, bleeding into red and eventually cooling off for green and blue near the top…

At least, once upon a time.

Now, just the stone base and shattered fragments of colour remained.

"You know the palace well," Lefios said as he hurried to keep up. "All of your memories of where to search… did you spend a lot of time here, as a poet?"

"My family had rooms on the grounds – connected to the main buildings."

"Your family?"

"Lefios, tell me something. Are you expecting to survive this?"

The man paused.

Vilas did not stop walking.

Hurried footsteps followed, joined by the clicking of his cane, and once Lefios was alongside once more, he gave his answer – which was another question. "Are you not?"

"I will leave this city."

"Your unfinished business."

Vilas nodded.

"Then, what of your question to me? Could it be, are you asking me to flee before you... I'm not sure. Raze the palace, instead of freeing the Spring?"

He almost smiled. "Is that what you think?"

"I don't know what to think," the man replied. He did not continue right away. "But to answer you, I *am* expecting to return. For now, I don't see any reason for the queen to remove me, if that's what you've been wondering."

"I see."

"Kivora occupies my thoughts more. When we first met, I did not see any hint that her end goal was the Spring, let alone that she might be able to restore it."

"Suggesting that a Shadow Radiant or Luminary is the one with something up their sleeve?"

"I wonder about that. And it always brings me back to the Brutes. How is she controlling them? *Is* she controlling them? I worry that I've misjudged the full extent of her abilities."

Now Vilas slowed, coming to a halt when sunlight struck a pale arch, one that would lead to the greenhouse. "Power over the Brutes. Meaning, power over their corpses?"

He leant against his cane with a nod. "Is it possible? Could the Brutes have entombed themselves at the lake, and she actually resurrected them?"

Vilas exhaled. "I admit, I've always assumed that the Brutes went into hibernation. Not death. If she can control them, she is requiring their labour only – to clear the blockage. And if that is true, how does it feed into all of her actions so far? Not to mention the Wahkyog themselves."

"Kivora might not have total power over them," he replied. "She might have lost control of one or a few, at different times."

"Agreed. But if you're thinking of the massacre, that sounds like the Davorian."

"Likely, yes. But I meant the Brute at the dam."

The woman continued to grow as a threat. *Enough to actually stop me?* "There was that bird's nest too, with the unbroken eggs." He frowned. "When we meet the others, we need to go over everything we know about Kivora."

Chapter 25.

Vilas stood within the Grand Greenhouse – an empty, stretching garden of wide tiers. All were dirt and stone, save for the one they stood upon. It also bore blackened scorch marks that would never fade, and like the lower tiers, its latticework of glass and steel had been reduced to little more than thin fingers extending toward each other, unlikely to meet again.

Flakes of rust drifted down on a soft breeze as he stared.

Once, it had been home to all manner of trees, plants and flowers – a place where insects danced in pollen…

If nothing else, the dark mountains were unchanged where they overlooked the palace.

In better news, the trail of the Brutes was finally clear. Cracked stone and deep footprints in the slag and blackened earth led toward the Spring of Nectar, guarded within ancient caverns at the base of the mountain walls. From where he stood, it waited just out of sight, since the greenhouse sloped down.

Would they be met with rubble only?

For Kivora, the Brutes and any others she had brought along, she'd face the same problem. Or already had done so. *I could still be wrong about that – she might not be there at all.*

"Vilas, take two Bindings, if you need them," Tano said.

The Radiant stood nearby, having moved quietly. *Either that or I was too lost in thought to notice. Again.*

Embers were already flowing toward Vilas. A warmth rose within, one that burned away some of his sombre mood. And even that was a surprise, for the churn of grief, bitterness and anger that he'd carried since arriving, it all should have lingered.

Fire brought focus?

"I will need this, and perhaps more."

He nodded. "You shall have it, if you ask."

"Thank you, Tano," Vilas replied. *A welcome development.* He gestured toward the canyon walls. "Do you feel ready for what is to come?"

"Not in the way I would like."

"Doubts?"

"Not about your abilities, no," he said. "If the Brutes attack, I know your Embers will stop them. It is Kivora and the Shadow Radiant. Assuming there is only one."

"How would you usually face them?"

"What we can Bind in stone, steel or wood, cannot

be Bound in flesh – I assume you knew that much?"

"Yes."

"Well, that does hold true – unless it is another Radiant. One on one, I have been able to Bind any and all. Only the Luminaries working in tandem are too strong for me."

As expected of his reputation, yet still impressive. "And the Shadow Radiants?"

"If I Bind one, another can undo my work. If only Tiliana is there, I believe I could Bind her easily enough, but in time, she would be able to break free."

"You are not alone in what is to come."

"Nor will they be. After all, there is whoever commands, Kivora herself, and one other I'm expecting."

"The Fang."

He nodded.

"I imagine Yadira would be faster, if that helps."

"It does." The man chuckled. "You know, I appreciate this. Perhaps especially from the Beast of Khiya."

"And now you're wondering what has brought this on?"

"Frankly, yes."

Vilas scratched at stubble on his cheek. "There is no particular reason, save to say that much depends on what happens next. We all want to survive."

"We do."

He seemed about to say more, but Lefios and Yadira approached. "We are prepared, well as we can be," she said.

"Then let's discover what Kivora has in store for us," Vilas replied, leading them across blackened ground that rose in a modest hill… and there he nearly faltered, struck by a memory.

Children had once rolled down soft grass, shrieking with laughter, calling for the adults to catch them before they tumbled into what had once been a shallow pool. *Everywhere I turn.* He let the Embers smother a flash of fury that followed.

No attacks came as they crested the hill, allowing an unobstructed view of the cavern-mouth, which lay open before them. "No surprise, perhaps," he said.

The rockslide had been cleared away; tossed to either side or simply scattered about the place, creating a maze of rubble. Shadows lurked within the cavern, but enough of the tiled floor inside remained visible to note deep cracks in the white.

Farther in, presumably, waited the Nectar Well and the source of the Spring.

Providing that it, too, had not been buried in stone back when the princess poisoned it. Doubts resurfaced. Kivora and the others had *something* up their sleeve. *Did they dig down to remove Taranera's skeleton?* Unlikely, surely?

"Are they all inside, then?" Tano asked as he stared down, arms folded.

"Most likely."

Yadira was stretching her legs, catching one foot at a

time as she bent her knees back behind her body. Her blue eyes were a little icy now. "The moment I have a target, I will strike. They will barely see me, but I need assurances."

"Meaning?" Vilas asked.

"That if the Spring has already been restored, that you will not simply bury the entire mountainside with the Embers of Maelohas."

"I have given Queen Ima my word."

"Good."

"We do need at least someone alive, too," Tano added. "Her Majesty won't be satisfied unless we can be certain the threat is finished."

"She said as much to me as well," Yadira added.

Vilas started down the slope, his steps no longer heavy. Purpose and power flowed through his limbs. "If killing Kivora doesn't stop the Brutes, then leave them to me," he said, flames now escaping his mouth.

Chapter 26.

"Finally." Vilas exhaled when they entered the dim cavern, more flames escaping as he did.

A dozen figures stood silent upon the white tiles, their bodies obscuring the view of a pale well, shaped as a blossoming lily. Faint fumes hung within the air but did not seem to be troubling those who waited.

None of which were Brutes.

Kivora stood in her usual furs, the Shadow Radiant Tiliana beside her, clothed in dark robes with a swirling pattern of white on the hem. They were joined by two other figures that were clearly Luminaries, from their clean white robes and torch-symbols.

Meveto and another Luminary, someone Vilas did not recognise.

The rest of the group was made up of Cherished Sons – but the cultists did not move, did not even respond when Kivora pushed through them, Tiliana in tow.

"Welcome, Vilas and friends." The Davorian smiled. And while it was void of warmth, it was not a cold smile, either. Instead, suppressed excitement threatened to escape. And maybe it did, considering the brightness of her eyes.

"Where are your pets?" he asked.

"Not far," she replied, and if nothing else, the woman confirmed that she had been controlling the Wahkyog.

"Does it matter? You have failed," Tano said, though he was frowning at Tiliana. "The Spring may be uncovered, but it is still poisoned."

"I do have a solution to that, now that the Beast has finally arrived," Kivora said.

Vilas let the fire flare in his eyes and mouth. "Oh?"

"While I didn't end up needing your power to clear a way, you're still useful. You're going into the well, where your death will purify the Spring. Isn't that right, Meveto?"

The old man smiled, his lips appearing thin, cheeks gaunt now – even the torch tattoos on his skin were faded, in contrast to the one sewn into his clothing. "Just so. When he becomes *eviha*, he will purify the Spring and thereby undo the work of that Maelohas whore."

Vilas narrowed his eyes. "It will be that simple, will it?"

Kivora gestured to Tiliana. "Bind him."

The Shadow Radiant lifted her arms. Stone cracked

as it snapped into place around Vilas' legs, reaching his knees. *Unexpected.* Especially after the little chat with Tano, which had focused on the Shadow Radiant's ability to *un*bind.

Something Tano could not do. And yet, such things did not matter. All it would take was –

Stone crashed to the ground at the entry.

Vilas glanced back. Shapes had burst from the ground, fragments and hunks of stone still flying, revealing huge figures with dark skin of granite.

Their bodies were easily thrice as tall as Vilas himself, the span of their shoulders four times his own – and questing across the bulging biceps, across their entire bodies, really, were orange and blue markings. Not quite tattoos, not quite veins… but definitely aglow in the dim cavern.

And in a further, obvious contrast to the piece of hand found back at the dam, these Wahkyog were alive.

Or perhaps not – they are moving. *But they do not live.*

Their blocky, human-esque faces were slack, mouths agape to reveal dark tongues of blue – and their eyes were utterly, utterly empty where the Brutes towered above, blocking escape as the half-dozen creatures strode closer.

Somehow, Kivora *was* controlling them; they were now her Thralls.

"Can you risk a cave-in here, Vilas?" the woman asked, one hand upon her hip. "You may or may not care about your companions, but you don't want to accidently kill yourself now, do you?"

"You are right." Vilas called the Embers, but did not have them come screaming forth, instead, he focused on the tiles beneath the Brutes. They swiftly turned yellow, orange and then back to white – and with the Second Binding already released – a blue that soon caused cries from those around him to echo.

He absorbed the heat, having no trouble protecting everyone.

Mute still, the dead Wahkyog instantly sank to their chests, trapped before Kivora could holler more commands.

The Embers vanished. He flinched back, twisting in place as his collar constricted – Meveto and the other one. Vilas managed to choke out Tano's name, but the Radiant seemed locked in a silent struggle against Tiliana.

A curse upon the Luminaries!

Vilas raged against the collar, but it was no use – it never was. If not for the stone encasing his legs, he'd barely be able to stand, his breath already ragged.

But he managed to signal to Yadira.

She was already moving.

Through tears of pain that blurred his vision, he saw her armoured form streak forward like a lightning bolt made of steel. She reached the Luminaries so fast that her sword was a mere flash. Red burst free, splashing down both sets of robes as the two collapsed into a heap.

Vilas straightened, even as Kivora snarled.

The Embers rushed back within reach, banishing the pain as he called them to his feet. Rock melted away and he approached Kivora with a grin, kicking liquid-stone free from his legs, the drops hissing.

Tiliana had stumbled to her knees, but the Davorian did not even glance aside from where she stood behind her group of slaves – instead, the woman cried out. "Give up, Beast!" She glared across at Yadira. The Steel Maiden held her bloody blade ready but had not attacked. *Why?*

Kivora was still speaking. "I have the others. Stay where you are."

He turned.

A single surviving Brute had pulled itself from the cooling magma. Despite missing hips and legs, it lay on the tiles, outstretched arms quite elongated, and one hand each had encircled both Tano and Lefios.

And though they beat at the mighty grip, struggling to breathe while they fought, neither could break free.

All under Kivora's direction.

Somehow, even with her mistaken belief about exactly how the *eviha* worked, she'd managed to create a convincing stalemate.

"Into the well and I let them go," Kivora said. "I'll have no need to kill them, then. They can flee back to Onath for all I care."

Vilas shook his head. Queen Ima might forgive the loss of Lefios but not Tano's death. *No half-measures now.* The victory over Kivora and the Brutes needed to be convincing, if he was going to play his final card within Ima's bedchamber.

"How can I trust you?" For while Kivora was right about not being able to simply blast the cavern and everything inside it into tiny, molten pieces, he could use the Embers in more than one way. A little more time would be enough… but could Tano and Lefios afford that?

Kivora sneered. "I hold their lives in the palm of my hand."

Vilas glanced at Yadira, who appeared equally uncertain of their next move.

Something shimmered near the well.

The Devorian pitched forward. Light vanished from her eyes with alarming swiftness as she slumped to her knees, then toppled down, face smacking into the stone where she lay still.

A dagger protruded from her back, blood not yet blossoming through her furs.

Gasps of relief echoed from behind Vilas; the Brute had released Tano and Lefios, the creature crumbling into halves, no longer moving. At the same time, Kivora's row of Cherished Sons were tumbling to the tiles with thuds.

Of the queen's enemies, only Tiliana remained breathing, and it did not seem as though she were about to rise.

Vilas kept the Embers at his fingertips. *Who else is*

here?

The air where the Devorian had once stood shimmered again. And then, it seemed to split – revealing a figure clad in grey and black. Even his hands and feet were wrapped... to keep movements quiet, it seemed. The shimmering in the air continued to fall away as the figure raised a hand, perhaps to push back a hood?

An Onathian was revealed.

It seemed that the shimmering moved not unlike fabric – some sort of magic cloak, then.

The man was old enough to carry his share of wrinkles and silver streaked its way through black hair and beard, his dark eyes impassive as he spoke. "Lord Tano, would you also secure the prisoner's hands, if you are sufficiently recovered." He paused to address Vilas next. "Vilas, Beast of Khiya, I am Osidani, known as the old king's Fang, and I wish your assistance with my interrogation of the traitor."

Chapter 27.

The cavern now seemed to be scattered with a number of corpses to equal the stones.

Gathered together a short distance from the magnificent well, which held only a vast pool of purple sludge below, the Fang paced while Tiliana spoke. Everyone else listened; Tano while keeping a grip on the Bindings, and with the occasional confused glance at the Fang, Lefios wearing a frown and Yadira sitting upon one of the large hunks of rock.

Vilas stood, arms folded.

"No," the Shadow Radiant shook her head. "I am certain that Kivora worked with only a small faction from her homeland – something she was quite bitter about. More were to join us in the mountains, but they did not arrive. That's why she went through so many Cherished Sons."

Lefios' frown deepened.

"Should that not prove to be true, you will have

forfeited your life," the Fang told her.

"It is true," she said, speaking firmly.

"I hope it so. While I presume that Luminary Meveto and Luminary Lunet provided the Devorian with knowledge about the city and Maelohas, I will need names of the others."

Tiliana smiled. "Anyone with the title of Luminary as a prefix."

The Fang stopped. "All?"

"Near enough. Only Hoen, since they mistakenly believe him to be too stupid to be of use."

"That is a lie," Tano said. "Sharila, especially, would never betray the queen."

"You are wrong."

The Fang glanced between them. "Explain, Tiliana."

"Obviously, they despise the changes Queen Ima is making. They want a return to the time of her grandfather – you know all of this, right?"

"Specifically?"

The woman shrugged. "So many things. Her steps toward social equality and religious freedom for one. Her plans to outlaw the use of all Maelohas items. Even her plans to formally acknowledge the death and destruction of Khyia as a mistake. As far as they're concerned, it's all a reduction of their own power, and they hate her for it – helping Kivora allowed them to work against the queen via proxy."

Vilas raised an eyebrow as he listened. *That was something I had not expected.*

"Go on," the Fang said.

"If they succeeded here, they would have used such a triumph to win over the rank and file, or simply destroy Queen Ima and her allies in order to begin anew. The death of the Beast in this place was another victory in their minds, since their research had failed and they were getting too old. They were desperate enough to try once again, to restore the Spring."

"And what of you?" Vilas asked.

She shrugged. "I wanted what a few of them are yet to admit – life."

"Long life."

"Yes."

"Explain that belief," the Fang said. His gaze had not softened.

The Shadow Radiant met his gaze. "You are not well informed, for some reason."

He sighed. "Is that all you can imagine?"

"What do you mean?"

Yadira waved a hand. "He's attempting to verify your words, to see if they match with what he already knows, of course. And if you want to earn your freedom, you should just answer him."

"Fine," she replied with a glower. "From all the research completed on Vilas, all the failures to recreate what was unique to the Maelohas, the Luminaries came to believe the Spring of Nectar had to be restored, as I said."

"And they believed it possible, how?"

"By casting a living Maelohas into the source. Their failed research on the *eviha* led them to believe it was possible. They were happy that Kivora and the Brutes functioned as an excuse to send Vilas out into the world."

Vilas glared. "They could have taken me here at any time."

"Not so, Beast," she replied. "Meveto in particular was adamant about secrecy. They could not just take you to this place without Queen Ima becoming aware and interfering. Subterfuge was deemed best. I agreed."

"Even if they'd succeeded, would the Spring have helped them?" Lefios asked.

Tiliana shrugged. "Partaking of the Spring day to day, drinking from the wells, eating of the food produced from the rivers, living in the city would grant access to such wonders."

"Would that be enough?"

"According to certain history books, yes. They claimed that even foreigners could benefit, though to a lesser extent."

The Fang turned to Vilas.

"Yes," he explained. "That was one reason visitors could not live here too long. Several years was usually the most allowed."

Tiliana sneered. "Hoarding a powerful resource that could benefit all."

"I have heard such an excuse for genocide many times."

"Pah."

"I'm surprised to hear you bother with the pretence

that 'Luminaries' would actually share such a gift."

"Isn't there some truth to what she is saying?" Yadira asked.

Vilas sighed. How many times had he gone through such things with Radiants and nobles over the decades? *Usually the younger ones, convinced they had all the answers. All the disgusting little justifications.* "Is it hoarding to protect people from grief?"

"How so?"

"Yadira, it is obvious. When a visitor resided in Khiya too long, they outlived all of their loved ones. *Anyone* they once knew. They lost connections to their past, to places, and so they were cut adrift."

Tiliana struggled to her feet, but she could not take a single step. "Liar! What of people who simply wanted a better life? They could have benefited from the Spring." Her voice was rising. "And what if they had *none* of the things you mentioned in their homelands? Illnesses that could not be cured at home? What if they were already suffering? Didn't you greedy bastards ever consider that?"

"You pathetic little fool," Vilas said, keeping his voice even. "The greed of *your people* destroyed such a place."

"What?"

"Do you even know of our priests?"

She did not answer.

"Healers. Healers in Khiya who welcomed all, and

who travelled the lands – or they did, before being hunted so that *your people* could harvest their bodies," he snapped. "And is your mind so addled with the lies told to you as a child that you can hardly even imagine change?"

"I –"

"Imbecile! Khiya was never given a chance to change. The people who ruled, or those that came after, might have changed the policy for visitors, might have made exceptions for all I know but instead, the greed of *your people* slaughtered and devoured my own."

Tiliana swallowed, shaking her head as she did.

"No more," the Fang said. "I need answers, not theatrics."

Vilas took a step toward the assassin, flames escaping from his mouth once more. "Are you sure that is the best word to use right now?"

The man hesitated, doubt clear in his gaze, and he raised both hands. "You are right. The traitor is my concern."

"Grant me exile," Tiliana replied, her gaze still fierce.

"I cannot make that decision."

"Kill me, then. I have nothing else to say."

"Lord Osidani, Queen Ima gave me explicit orders to return with a captive for her own interrogation," Tano said.

"Of course," he replied.

"Depending on what else she can tell us, I imagine

exile might still be an option."

The Fang nodded, then pointed at Tiliana. "You have my word, traitor. I will request as much of Her Majesty, but you will have to convince Queen Ima yourself, when the time comes."

"Fine."

"Good enough. That Davorian's plan. Tell me, would the Spring have been cleansed?"

"That's what Luminaries promised. The Beast would have died, and transformed into something called *eviha* and in time, purified the Spring at its source."

The Fang looked to Vilas again.

"No."

Osidani raised an eyebrow, as Tiliana glared.

"Only from self-sacrifice can *eviha* come. And only if buried for years. Had these fools simply cast me into the well, or coerced me to leap within via false promises, I would have died, and that is all."

"He's lying, again," Tiliana said.

Vilas ignored her, instead speaking to Fang. "Just because the Luminaries were mistaken, that does not mean that they did not come close to the truth, and in the process, reveal their hand."

"So it seems."

"What of the Brutes?" Tano asked in the silence that followed.

"All dead, as you've probably guessed," Tiliana said with a shrug. "They did not all survive the journey.

And they were never alive to begin with, for that matter. Kivora was controlling them, as best she could."

"As best she could?"

"Sometimes one or two would break free and… act alone, even though she assured me they had all died long ago."

"Like the one at the dam," Tano said.

"Yes."

Meaning that one of them most likely had *taken the time to protect that bird's nest in the forest.* More cruelty committed by the Davorian, who woke the last remnants of a race and then forced them to commit acts of astounding evil.

"Are there more?" Vilas asked.

"No," she said. "She tried to find and wake others, but she could not."

"How was she doing this?" Tano glanced back toward the stony corpse of the Brute that had held him. "Could someone else repeat that?"

"If you mean a fellow Cleaver or a Luminary, then I don't believe so. But Kivora knew something from long before we met."

"Then another, someone from Davora could possibly try the same thing again."

Lefios nodded, almost to himself.

"I don't know." Tiliana lowered herself back to the cracked and broken tiles with a sigh of weariness. "She complained of how long it took to find even the few Brutes we *could* locate."

"I believe Queen Ima will be pleased with what we have learned so far." Yadira hopped down from her perch, armour clanking. "But I think it best to continue this outside – faint as they are, those fumes cannot be good for any of us."

Tano nodded. "Sound advice. We'll continue the interrogation on the path home."

"Where our pet Shadow Radiant can explain how they survived the Anchored Spirits," Vilas added.

She did not respond.

"I have something that may assist, also," the Fang added, without elaborating.

Tano nodded, though he did not seem to be in a hurry to leave, not easing the Bindings on Tiliana or addressing her at all. "Lord Osidani, I am pleased to discover that your loyalties lie with the queen."

The Fang worked to fold the impressive cloak into his pack, creating unsettling deformations to what was visible. "It lies with the nation, Lord Tano. And for now, Queen Ima is the only leader unwilling to deal in treachery – something that cannot be said about her grandfather. Or the Luminaries."

"I see. That is a relief, nevertheless," he replied, his tone a little uncertain.

The man paused. "She did not inform you that I had my own task?"

"Our conversation was more general in nature."

"Ah." He nodded. "To perhaps put your mind somewhat at ease, I believe that Her Majesty wanted to keep one final card up her sleeve, in case Lefios was still working with the Davorian."

Tano's expression did suggest at least some relief. "Ah."

And it was clear once again, that Ima was not to be underestimated.

Chapter 28.

Vilas stood in Queen Ima's bedchambers, bare feet sinking into the carpet, lamplight gleaming on the wall of windows before him. Its glass would be reinforced by Bindings, of course, but the windows were also noteworthy in their arrangement, curving like waves along the wall.

He did not bother to question the design choice as he let his tunic fall to the floor, leaving his pants as the last item of clothing now, and instead staring down at the city.

Soon enough, you'll be just a pile of ash.

The long ride back to the city was already a faint memory; fifty years of imprisonment were about to come to an end.

Fifty years. Of isolation, of tests, of grieving, of reading and researching and learning everything he could about his captors. Of everything he had then weathered while chasing the Brutes, it all led to this very moment; a moment he would enjoy like no other.

For as much as Ima herself had filled his dreams, so did a revenge delayed, a revenge he was never certain he would be able to savour. It had always been a glimmering carrot that dangled well within sight but just out of reach.

Perhaps a kind of desperate, pathetic lie he could tell himself in order to keep breathing.

Until now.

Now, it was finally time to discover the truth about all he had read and prepared, to see what the queen's power could truly do.

Footsteps approached, and soft, gloved hands came to rest on his shoulders, trailing across the bare skin of his chest, the scent of orange and vanilla as much a tell as her gloves. "I was impressed by the way you handled Tano's disappointment earlier," he said.

"He understands," she replied.

"If so, he would be the only Radiant to do so. Hosun appeared close to biting through his own tongue."

Ima laughed. "They have no choice, and by the time Tano and Lord Osidani, among others, have finished with their own work this night, no-one will be willing to complain."

He rested a hand upon one of hers, his pulse quickening. "A reign of terror, Your Majesty?"

"Temporary."

"Don't all tyrants lie to themselves in that way?"

Her cool lips pressed against the back of his shoulder.

"Perhaps."

"Then, you are satisfied that I lived up to my end of the bargain? You will free me from this collar?"

"I am *very* pleased, Vilas. The Davorian and her Brutes are finished, and I have a talkative prisoner delivering all manner of names – such as the true identify of Asp."

"Oh?"

"Yes. I believe you may know him as Lord Noriam."

"I do," he said with a nod. Perhaps not a surprise, in the end. "Then, you've cornered him?"

"Noriam has fled the city, but his days are numbered." She slid her lips up to the back of his neck and he shivered. "More importantly, I've finally been able to confirm something astounding, after a long, long search. My enemies stand upon their final legs. I am happy."

What exactly did she consider 'astounding'? But he asked a different question, since of those enemies, one in particular interested him. "Including your grandfather, I presume?"

Her voice darkened. "His crimes will end soon enough."

"Then I earned my freedom."

"Yes. But you have a simpler reward to receive first." She turned his chin with two fingers, and her dark eyes were expectant. "Satisfy me and I will have the collar removed the very moment you have replaced your clothing, Beast."

"When you will face me as an enemy, Ima." He met her expectant gaze. "You know what I plan."

"Of course. You have spoken of little else my entire life – thirty-four years, and all I have heard is that you will take your revenge on the city," she replied with a smile.

Vilas smiled, then drew her close, pressing his own lips against hers.

She returned his kiss, her tongue brushing against his lips, then pulled back. "Follow me."

Ima wore only a short, sheer nightgown of the faintest pink, its hem twirling as she led him across the carpet and to the shadows of her bed. There, the lamplight gleamed on a pitcher of wine and two glasses. She took a sip from one glass and handed him the other.

Vilas drank sweet wine from his own, then replaced the glass. "Let's finish this later."

"Impatient, I see." But she replaced her wine and lay across the bed, taking him into her arms. Vilas ran his lips across her neck, taking soft bites of smooth skin when she murmured encouragement. He reached down to lift her gown, sliding it up from her hips, over her stomach to reveal her breasts, which he leant over, seeking her nipples with his mouth.

"Keep going," she soon told him, putting gentle but firm pressure on his shoulders.

He ran his tongue down her stomach, then moved to the inside of her thigh, trailing one hand across her other knee, before moving between her legs and sliding his tongue slowly against lips already wet with lust.

She moaned and her voice was enough to have him groan in response – and it was not only his cock, but his whole body that was growing hard; the sweet tension of anticipation overtaking him.

Ima caught his hair with one hand. She pushed his face deeper, wrapping both her legs around him as her moans grew – and then the queen pulled him up with a grin. "Roll over, Beast." He did so, letting her sit on his chest, her gloved hands drifting across his face. "Now, get rid of those pants."

He opened his mouth to run his tongue across her fingertips as he worked, hands moving far more deftly than he could have imagined, and then she slid back, lining up her hips with his where she paused, the heat from her body pouring into his. "Ready, Beast?"

Vilas nodded. "I have *waited* for this."

"Good." She reached down to guide him inside, grinding her hips against him – slowly at first, her mouth parted enough that he wanted to lean up and kiss her again.

Nothing had ever felt so good. Nothing. Not after *decades* without anyone to share his bed.

Without even being touched by a woman.

And nothing would, not until the shock of her hands hit him, and he'd finally be free of the collar… but even thoughts of his old plan were fleeting, a feather drifting on wind; he could not follow it, he *had* to lose himself to the pleasure.

Nothing else could matter.

Vilas matched her rhythm, steadily speeding up.

Their breathing soon became more ragged.

Pleasure and pressure swirled within him, and by the way that Ima's knees gripped him, she was nearing her climax too – he slapped both hands around her hips but did not try to control her movement…

… and fire consumed him.

Everything burned so slowly. Time softened. His body floated, passing through her scent, circling her smile, her gaze impossible to break and the collar upon his throat simply melting away. Embers surged through him; a vast power that he had only touched once before, at the Eastern Gate, where thousands and thousands of soldiers vanished in an instant of fire.

And then…

Freedom.

He blinked. Somehow, he was still in Ima's bed – he hadn't actually floated away to a wonderful 'elsewhere'. The queen rose from beside him, moving to another room on silent feet, her exquisite form a picture of grace. *Where is she going?* And did it matter? For when he reached up to his throat – the collar was truly gone!

Vilas swallowed freely, as if for the first time.

Go, quickly.

There was no time to enjoy the sensation. Vilas snatched up his pants, withdrew the tiny piece of *eviha* he'd saved, and crumbled his final safeguard into Ima's wine before rising to call for her.

The queen returned from an adjoining room, holding a long dagger in the one hand that no longer bore a glove. "Well?"

He rose to offer the wine, glancing at the blade – she would not be quicker than the Embers, which remained close. "Well what, Your Majesty?"

She accepted the glass in her gloved hand with a smile, taking a long drink, her gaze not leaving his own. "You must feel different."

"Of course," he said. "My heritage is no longer set beyond my reach, no longer something I must petition for. I feel alive again, as I have only felt a few times since my imprisonment."

"And your goal?"

"The explosion at the gates will be nothing compared to what I will do," he replied, softly. "You have time to escape, if you wish."

"My, how kind. Why don't you try, Vilas? Call your Embers."

He frowned at her. *Far too calm.* She'd done or arranged for something to happen – but no Radiants seemed to be nearby. And even if they were, the collar was gone now, melted beneath the heat of their passion – her power and his had combined to free him. *Exactly as I'd hoped.* "What do you mean?"

"Humour me."

Vilas pulled more power close, a beautiful warmth… and despite the tremendous surge from mere moments ago, he held nothing more than what he'd been able access with *two* Bindings released.

Maybe three.

A chill sapped his strength. His arm faltered, wine spilling to the carpet. "What is this?"

"I read the old tomes too, Vilas – everything you read, and more." The queen pointed her blade at him. "You were right to gamble on our union being enough to destroy the collar, but your arrogance clouded your judgement. Surely you must be aware that I know my own body? There is also a *cost* to sharing my bed, and I am relieved that you seem to have paid it."

"No."

"You can no longer destroy the city as you'd planned," she said. "I have burned away enough of your gift now. Surrender, Vilas. Surrender and I will find a meaningful use for you."

He did not answer. *How can this be?*

"Give up your inhumane desire for vengeance and join me. Help me *build* something. I don't believe that life should be wasted. You deserve more."

Her voice was earnest for all its strength – she actually believed her own words, it seemed. And yet, both her offer and compliments struck a wall; he did not blink.

She had not won, not yet.

There is still a way.

Vilas let his shoulders slump a little as he frowned at her, taking to care to affect some defiance to his tone. "I could still reduce the palace to rubble, one wing at a time, you know."

"But you'll be captured again, and your revenge spoiled," she replied. "Vilas, join me on the bed. Listen, now." She finished her wine and gestured for him to lead the way.

Does she already believe I might surrender? I have time, either way. He strode back to the bed and lay across the pillows.

Ima joined him, her head resting on one of his arms, her blade cool against his navel. The handle was still held firmly in her grip – bare skin close to his own. "Hear me, Vilas, for I have a fair vision." She spoke then of Khiya, in much the same way as the Fang had revealed, and of her plans for the city, of how to make Onath a better place. And while her ideals were quite grand, her ideas did seem practical.

As she spoke, a warmth continued to grow in her tone. Ima sounded happy. She even laughed, and at times her voice became almost girlish, such was her joy at the vision she had for the future, again, including things the Fang had revealed and more.

"Vilas, I even have a surprise for you. Something wonderful."

"You do?" He smiled. How much of her joyful candour came from the *eviha*, how much from Ima herself?

No matter, it's obviously taken hold.

Vilas placed a gentle hand upon her back. "Ima, I believe it is time for me to leave."

"Oh?"

He rose, careful as he helped her into a sitting position. He kissed her softly, then pulled back to stroke her cheek. "You should rest here."

"Well…" She glanced at the pillows. "It has been a long day. Let's continue talking, once you return."

"Of course." He stood and began to dress.

She sighed, her contentment drifting from the bed. "Vilas?"

"Yes?" He had already replaced pants and tunic. All that remained were socks and shoes, and then to slip away, taking the same discreet passages the queen had used to bring him to her rooms to begin with.

And then, a horse or carriage to Otakom Pass Dam.

Would she wake in time to make another move against him? *Or an escape, at least.*

"When will you return?" Ima asked.

"Soon."

Chapter 29.

Sneaking from Queen Ima's chambers, helping himself to several small ornamental sparrows of gold and a pair of fine sapphire earrings, escaping the palace itself by melting his way through a half-concealed wall in one of the gardens, striding along darkened streets in stolen cloak and hood, finally locating a carriage service – only to have the driver balk at payment, found what little patience Vilas had left sorely tested.

"It is a long trip. That I understand." He strove to keep his voice calm. "But you do not hold fool's gold, as I think we both know."

The driver returned the ornaments, a frown upon his weathered face. "It's not that. I simply don't have time to haggle with a money-changer when we return. And I can't spend them on the trip, nor on the way back."

Vilas produced the sapphire earrings. "Well?"

Now the man sighed after barely a glance. "You trying to get me executed? Only stuff that nice comes from the palace, or some rich noblewoman. I won't ask questions, but I need stalks or teeth. Same as everyone else."

"So be it. Where *is* the nearest money-changer?" Other carriages would likely respond in a similar fashion, which meant finding some currency.

"Open at this time?"

"You are taking customers."

He patted the door of his carriage with its deep green paint and brass trim. "I provide a reputable service that knows no limits of time."

Vilas sighed. But was there not another way? "A moment, and I will return."

"Not to worry, I have no other customers tonight. Yet."

Vilas strode to a nearby alleyway, muttering to himself as he did. Light from an upper storey spilled down to illuminate a series of barrels with steel bands. A shaggy dog lifted its head a moment, only to settle back in between the barrels with a snort.

Time to improvise.

He put the two golden sparrows back into a pocket, leaving the slightly larger ornament in his palm – a small goblet. Then, he called the Embers closer, pulling their warmth into his body, into his hands, and pushing it down to the gold and holding until the goblet melted. Then, he used a finger to split the shape into an approximation of Onathian currency, absorbing the heat to let the pieces cool.

The detail was not there, no Onath markings, but the shape was adequate.

Would it be enough to satisfy the driver?

If nothing else, using his gift would not have alerted the Radiants – without a collar to rely on, they could no longer trace him. Ima would still mobilise the entire city, be they Radiant, soldier or citizen, but not before she recovered.

And *drinking* the *eviha* made for a stronger effect than breathing the haze.

Vilas returned to the driver, and handed over the still-warm but vaguely stalk-shaped gold. "Will this be easier to use on our journey?"

"Well…" The man hesitated, then shook his head with a chuckle. "Easier, yes. But not without some effort. Tell me something before I accept this job. You're not just any foreigner, are you?"

"No."

"You're that one, the prisoner."

"Yes."

The man sighed. "Very well, hop in and keep the curtains drawn. And if I manage to get you there, I'm going to need those earrings after all."

"Of course." Vilas climbed into the carriage to find clean seats of dark blue, complete with a small cupboard and shelf, presumably for food or drink. *Luxurious.*

He settled back and closed his eyes but did not let the creeping weariness overtake him.

Not until he was certain that the carriage was

actually leaving the city.

Yet once he'd peeked outside a few times to ascertain the correct general direction, it did seem that the driver wanted the payment enough to take what was a large risk.

And when the sound of the cobbles beneath the wheels switched to that of a paved highway, Vilas finally let a long sigh escape.

***

Otakom Pass Dam waited above. It was a pale mass of bluestone visible in glimpses between branches and leaves that surrounded Vilas where he leant against the carriage, gazing up at his target.

Tension tightened every muscle within his body. Even warmth from the Embers could not ease it fully. Part excitement, part impatience, part… what? *Doubts?* He snorted to himself, and circled the carriage to thank the driver.

The man was taking time to tend to his horses.

Vilas handed over the earrings. "I am curious as to why you agreed to drive me here."

"If I stop to think, it's the money for the most part," he said with a grin.

Vilas laughed. "Your honesty is refreshing."

"A little bit thinks that you deserve to go free, after what happened to your people. So, there's that, too," he said with a shrug, then moved around to climb up into his seat. "Anyway, I'll leave you to your journey. It's a long way to the border, so you'd better be good at hunting."

"I am," Vilas said, and waved the fellow off.

Then he turned back to the treeline and strode within, creeping toward the roar of the Lidasch River far below. He paused at the edge of concealment, crouching in a moss-covered clearing. Logs, half-consumed by green, seemed to rise from the ground, pine needles and other leaves scattered like cast-off garments.

While the distant dam wall and its flow gates still stood proud and colossal within the dark rock of the surrounding mountain range, the destruction he could cause with his strike would not equal that which he could have unleashed from the city centre – had his gift survived Ima unscathed.

Reduced or not, the Bindings on the dam wall would not be enough to stop him. He could break them, could tear into the very earth beneath the dam; there was nothing to stop him now.

But how disappointing that, unlike in his dreams, there was no white-hot fury.

Only a flat, cold determination.

At last, Onath would face consequences for its unfathomable crimes.

Chapter 30.

"Stop this, Vilas."

He spun.

Radiant Tano had entered the clearing. Leaves and smudges of dirt clung to his white robe, which also bore several rips. His expression was not one of anger, despite the sharpness to his command. Instead, the younger man's eyes revealed a weary sadness.

"It does not matter how you found me, Tano. You cannot stop this."

"We don't know that."

"I do."

"But I have to try," he said. "Only a monster would stand back and watch."

Vilas met the man's gaze. "Making me a monster, I suppose?"

"Yes." Tano only nodded. "But even monsters can change, I think."

"Oh?"

"You don't really want to do this, Vilas. You cannot possibly have seen the destruction in the city, seen for yourself the aftermath, the loss of all those innocents in Khiya, and now want to do the very same thing to the innocents below."

"It is not the same. And I will not be harvesting the dead."

"Just murdering the living."

"*That* is the price of choices Onath has made."

Tano spread his arms. "But Onath is not its past."

"I speak of its present, also," Vilas said with a frown. "After all, the city is always hungry, don't you think? Always seeking more flavour. Like the salt you make from our bones and teeth. Or the aphrodisiac from ground tongues and other organs – it's been called a few things over the years, but it's 'sting' these days, as I'm sure you know."

"I do, but –"

"Or the dried strips of our flesh and tendons – I remember certain athletes on a steady diet, in the early days after the genocide. I'm sure all those Anchored Spirits would be set to rest, if only they knew that a young woman, whose name I cannot recall, was announced as the fastest in all of Onath. What a bright day for her."

Tano did not answer; he barely had time, even if he'd planned to try again, as Vilas was not at all finished.

"Blood was used to heal the sick back then, too. But mostly, it was wasted on those ghouls you call

Luminaries – or royal pigs, like Ima's father and his father before him. Right away they knew it would not last, and even when your army went after the villages and little hamlets next, blood never lasted as long as our bodies, did it?" He'd clenched his hands into fists now. "Or our hair. Have you seen them, Radiant? The nobles who rush to parade through the sparkling streets of Onath, eager to show off their woven bracelets, convinced that in time, it will make them grow more beautiful."

"I have seen them."

"And how many stalks did the so-called 'Braid of the Last Priestess' sell for? Over ten thousand? Perhaps that one was also before your time, but there are a thousand stories like those I have shared."

"Enough," Tano said. "I know the crimes."

"And the lies, I'm sure. They've all been carefully preserved in those tomes that Radiants pass off to their young faithful as 'history'."

"Vilas, I'm aware of what was said. You aren't teaching – or convincing me. I know our leaders told lie after lie about your people being child-murderers, and a dozen other falsehoods for that matter. I know they manufactured the conditions for the assassination, I know they faked raids on Onathian villages and blamed it on Maelohas. I know the invasion was a pretext to take control of the Spring, and I know harvesting your people was considered an acceptable consolation." His voice wavered. "But there are so many down there –

including children, *Vilas*, that deserve to have a future."

"No-one offered the children of Khiya a future," he snapped. "Why should Onath have one?"

"You don't believe that!"

Vilas spoke through clenched teeth, flames already escaping his mouth, curling around his head, all without harming a single hair. "Yes, I do."

He dragged the Embers near, everything he could now muster as he faced the dam – and let them burst beneath his target.

Stone exploded.

Red magma followed, spreading like splayed hands as it hurled smouldering earth and rock into the air. Water shot forth too, hissing steam joined by a booming rumble that echoed across the mountains, near powerful enough to deafen.

Tano cried out but Vilas did not turn.

At last.

Cracks shot through the dam. All across the surface, the masonry broke away, torrents of water bursting forth. More, enormous hunks of rock broke free to tumble into the river, splashback nearly reaching Vilas where he stood, watching as the flow gates crumbled.

The upper chamber and top of the dam remained intact, Bindings holding for now, but only moments passed before its base finally gave way with a roar – swallowed by a wall of surging death, white water thrashing.

"No!"

Tano leapt forward, hands raised.

The very air above the river shimmered yellow. Water and stone crashed into the glow with an ear-splitting crack, and it held – the bulk of the flood was caught.

Bindings spread swiftly.

They dug down into the water itself, spearing into the hunks of visible wall and stone, sliding together slowly to create the beginnings of a new barrier. It had not stopped everything, but it would be enough to save the city!

Vilas growled.

The Bindings were still glowing. Tano slumped to his knees but had not given up – the Radiant was holding back the entire dam with his magic, water continuing to rise. Yet the more it climbed the sides of the gorge, the more Bindings shot forth in a myriad of directions, doubtless forging desperately onward.

"Very well done," Vilas said as he stalked over to Tano. *He can even Bind air, it seems. Ima's last gambit?* He kicked the Radiant to the earth. "But this is futile, Tano. I can obliterate the entire river and its banks at any point, wider and deeper than anything you have done."

"You aren't strong enough… anymore," he said without looking from his barrier.

"Let's find out."

Chapter 31.

Something sharp sliced the skin of his throat. A trickle of warm blood crept after, and the scent of steel and leather reached him at the same time – that, and sweat.

"Your life is in my hands."

Yadira.

Her words had been deceptively calm.

Vilas made no threatening movements, but nor did he release a hold on the Embers. He absolutely had enough to ensure the ground beneath their feet erupted in molten lava, to burn everything *around* him to cinders.

More, if needed, and if needed he would die himself, if that's what it took to wipe out the Bindings in the river.

But was he faster than the Steel Maiden?

"Yadira?" Shock filled Tano's voice.

"I never claimed that I had to survive my revenge," Vilas told her. "I will burn this entire forest, the river and every living thing inside down to the ground with my death."

"Not until you hear what I must say. I did not carry her all this way for nothing."

"Ima need not have bothered."

"No, Vilas. The queen sent me here so that you might meet someone. I doubt I will be able to pronounce her name properly. Will you meet her, before you make any decision?"

"I already made my decision." He kept himself still. *Be patient.* "Tano stopped it. Temporarily."

"Please. I have not misjudged you."

He hesitated at her words, and the unexpected catch to her voice. "Who are you talking about?"

"I will bring her, but don't forget that I truly am *much* faster than you," she said. "And try not to scare her, Vilas."

"Very well." Despite the fact that his revenge was caught in a delicate web of rapidly thinning strands, curiosity had its claws deep within.

Yadira withdrew the blade as she stepped back.

He turned as she strode around one of the larger trunks, moving mostly out of sight. But she seemed to be kneeling, speaking only softly.

No answer could he hear.

And when the Steel Maiden returned, it was with one hand resting lightly upon the shoulder of an older girl.

Her gaze flickered from person to person, uncertainty

clear in her tiny movements, in what seemed an unwillingness to draw attention. Yet of course she did; the girl wore borrowed clothes – well-made, but a little too large, and her dark hair was short, a ragged cut.

Her eyes were dark too, and unlike the Onathians, her skin was tanned.

Different to Yadira, too.

More like my own...

Vilas took half a step forward. Why had Yadira been uncertain about getting the name correct?

The worried girl met his gaze.

Something was different there. A cautious hope had entered her eyes, as though it were something she could not risk letting free.

"You are safe now," he said, the words spilling forth in Maelohas.

Her eyes widened, brimming with tears as she dashed forward.

Vilas knelt and took her into his arms.

Chapter 32.

Fira slept in Vilas' arms where he leant against one of the moss-covered logs in the clearing, her modest weight no burden at all.

Fira. Short for Firaluveka, and meaning *arc of light*.

Speaking of the hope her parents had for her, even while captive...

The girl slept deeply. She did not stir whenever he shifted his legs, nor when he occasionally lifted an arm to drink from the flask of water Yadira had provided.

A Maelohas girl.

A miracle.

A thousand questions remained. Some of which would not be answered until he stood before the queen once more – Ima, who had so neatly outsmarted him, and quite obviously saved Onath.

The simmering fury, the emptiness that had both fuelled *and* gnawed at him over decades, was easing. Hatred remained. He would *never* forgive the city, but its destruction was suddenly no longer paramount.

Fira had to be protected – had to be taken away from Onath.

They'd shared only little before she sought her rest. However, it had been enough for Vilas to exchange names and hear that, once her parents died, she'd assumed she was alone in the world, and he then knew beyond a doubt that Fira could not suffer another moment of harm, this girl he had barely met.

"How?" Vilas asked.

Yadira and Tano stood together nearby, discussing whatever it was, for who knew how long, since he'd barely spared either of them a glance. Not since Fira first repeated his name.

"I can answer at least some of your questions," Yadira offered. "What first?"

The Radiant joined her, his expression haggard, but he did not seem to carry any bitterness. *A better man than I.*

"Fira."

"You will have to seek the full story from Queen Ima, but when she gave me my task, she mentioned a suspicion that her grandfather had kept a terrible secret for many, many years."

Vilas narrowed his eyes. "Fira's family."

"I assume so, but when I rescued her, there were no signs of anyone else in that place. We assumed her parents had already died." She lowered her voice. "Possibly as a result of Radiant experiments."

Some of his fury began to creep back but he pushed it aside. *Not yet.* "When did Ima know?" After all, the queen often spoke of Yadira 'having her own task', or something similar enough.

"Since before we first visited the dam."

He shook his head, but it was in admiration, as much as anything else. "Tano, what about you?"

"Her Majesty does not share all of her goals with me, as I have come to learn."

Yadira slapped him on the shoulder. "She will now, hero."

The man actually smiled as he spread his hands. "Well…"

Perhaps Ima previously held concerns about Tano. After all, he could have harboured some hidden loyalty to the Luminaries. But whatever the case, she believed in the Radiant enough to have him chase after and then try to stop Vilas from destroying the dam.

Or, to cause a delay until Yadira arrived with Fira.

Vilas could not stop a frown at their celebrations, even such modest ones – by all measures, Tano, Yadira and Ima had indeed saved many, many lives. Many who were undeserving…

And what clearer proof that I failed my people?

Failed, despite actually taking a final desperate measure of his own. "Tano, had you always known you could set Bindings through air?"

The Radiant paused, then shook his head. "No. There are vague theories, but it was not known… before today.

Why do you ask?"

Vilas shrugged. "No real reason. Do either of you know what Ima plans to offer me?"

Both shook their heads, but the Radiant gestured to the dam. "Then you've given up on your revenge? If so, I will send a message to Risi and the others that it is safe to return and begin rebuilding."

"You warned them?"

"Of course."

Yadira sighed. "Vilas, I hope you are not actually disappointed to hear that."

He raised one hand, still moving gently, so as not to wake Fira. "My disappointment is for myself, and the fact that I was apparently so easily thwarted." He glanced down at Fira then and found himself with little else to say.

"None of what we've been through seemed easy to me," Tano noted.

Yadira nodded her agreement.

"And what now?" Vilas asked. "Your orders from Ima?"

The Radiant moved toward the barrier he had made, still taking slow steps. "I will assist those at the dam, for the time being."

"Yadira?"

She joined Vilas, leaning against the moss – and for the first time since they had met, Yadira removed her half-mask. She was, expectedly for a noblewoman, quite attractive, with fine features that could not undermine a stern gaze. "Vilas, I judged that something good had survived within you."

He did not know whether to frown or smile.

"It was not easily found. But in time, once I was certain, I shared my belief with the queen. That you could be redeemed – and most importantly to her, I suspect, that you were actually worthy of a chance to seek that redemption."

Vilas opened his mouth to answer, something about how he'd never needed the queen's permission to seek such a thing… but the truth was not so clear. Not now. It *had* been, not so long ago. The truth had been so clear that, in fact, he had no longer been able to see *beyond* it, in a troubling contradiction.

Who then, was the best judge of his deservedness?

No-one offered the children of Khiya a future. Why should Onath have one?

Words of bitter fury echoing within his mind.

Not another man's words, either.

Beliefs he would have to leave behind, somehow, even if the words did not repulse him as much as they could have.

"I cannot forgive the city."

She nodded. "Nor would I, honestly. But you chose destruction, and only Tano stopped it – and so, I will be watching you, Vilas. For the sake of this girl, as much as the people of Onath."

Chapter 33.

Once again, Vilas found himself within Ima's warm chambers, this time seated at a round table of rosewood. Generous lamplight set the surface and cutlery to gleaming, along with the meal of spiced soup that sat before them.

This time, Fira was included, and though she was old enough to possess a large vocabulary, she rarely spoke. Nor had she on their journey back, rarely letting Vilas from her sight. Even now, while focused on her food, she still looked up at times, as if to ensure he had not left the room.

Vilas found himself yet to touch his own spoon, having listened to the queen's words most intently. "I will think on your offers," he told her when she finished, and he had to admit to being tempted.

Trying to restore something of Khiya, something of his people – was it possible? *Could I actually work with Radiants, even those hand-picked by Ima?* An equal concern was Fira. What was best for the girl? She had never seen her homeland. The first view should not be of a poisonous ruin…

"Good." Ima smiled across the table. "If you have no further questions, I would hear more of the *eviha*. Since you had enough to drug me, I assume there is more?"

"No, but I do have more questions."

Though she frowned, the queen did gesture for him to proceed.

"Yadira was assessing me while we travelled. What if she had spoken in the negative?"

"Her orders were to kill or incapacitate you once the Brutes had been dealt with, of course."

He raised an eyebrow. Troubling honesty. And, after a fashion, bearing rather morbid similarities with her forebears.

"That is the truth, Vilas. I expect the same from you, if you want to provide a future for Fira."

"That is fair. And Tano?"

She chuckled. "I must admit, while luck played its part, Tano was entirely by design."

"Meaning?"

"Are you sure you need the very specific details of the ways I bested you, Beast?"

Vilas grinned. "I am."

The queen set her own cutlery to one side, leaning forward, elbows on the table so that she could rest her chin upon gloved hands. "So be it. Luck played a part in timing, firstly. I was closing in on my grandfather's secret without knowing the full extent of what I'd find, *before* the Brute was discovered. Once that happened, I knew I held the necessary excuse to let you out of your cage, and since Yadira was already visiting, I had someone trustworthy, someone beyond the machinations of the palace, to watch you."

"To see if I would be able to remove *all* the obstacles you were facing. Not just the Brutes, but your grandfather's faction too."

She nodded.

"And you needed someone swift enough to chase me down if I ran, I assume?"

"Very much so," Ima replied. "That speed was vital in more ways than one."

"How so?"

"For some of what I required of her, I would request that you ask Yadira yourself."

He nodded. *International intrigue? Or something else?*

"To satisfy your curiosity, by the time I finally located the cells grandfather had used for Fira, no-one else could reach and free the girl in time to then catch up to Tano, especially not while carrying a poor, frightened child all that way."

"Tano left first to delay me, if he couldn't stop me."

"Yes."

"He was right behind me, Ima – did he mark me when I left the palace?"

"Before our tryst, I asked him to be ready," she said,

with a nod. "If not for your little trick with the wine delaying *me*, you might not have escaped the palace grounds."

Vilas smiled. "We each knew as much about one another."

"Yes."

He lifted his spoon now and took a sip of the soup – the mix of spice and richness, of course, excellent. He also took a moment to smile at Fira. "How does this all relate to Tano being of your design?"

"By comparison. He was chosen, not just for his strength, but because *he* was the one with the best chance of succeeding with you."

"He was?" Vilas raised an eyebrow. "We did not exactly… enjoy our time together."

"Nor would you have with any."

"I imagine so."

"But can you deny the results of your time together?"

"At defeating Kivora and the Brutes, I cannot."

"Exactly, Vilas." She leant back now. "I was watching him for a long time. Most Radiants are not like Tano, and if you had been more mature, you would have seen that."

"Oh?"

Ima chuckled. "Yes, you pig-headed fool. In fact, I think you *did* recognise that Tano was pure of intent, at least on some level."

"Did I?"

"And if you took out anger upon him, it was precisely

because he was different to the other Radiants."

"I disagree."

She pointed. "Trust me. He didn't match the image you had constructed, one that isn't actually inaccurate for the most part; that of a bloodthirsty, cruel Radiant, one born of typical Onathian greed. But Tano was none of those things. He was not the enemy you needed on hand to remind you of the pain, to fuel the desire for such a hideous revenge. He was not easy to loathe, and you loathed him for that fact."

"I…" he trailed off.

Ima was wrong. Tano was…

Vilas stared into his soup, but nothing of use floated between the vegetables and slices of meat. Only his own deep frown, reflected back at him – not exactly petulant, but hardly the expression of someone who had enjoyed what they had been told, either.

Hardly the expression of an adult.

"Come now, Vilas. Tano is the perfect example of someone who did not deserve what you had in mind. A young man with no real links to what happened at Khiya, and someone that found such history utterly repulsive. Someone who would fight to stop it happening again, anywhere, to anyone," she said. "And you know that in this city today, he is one of many. You know who your true targets should have been, all along."

She was right.

Perfect for her plans. The damned Radiant *was* the best choice to start a long thaw of his hatred.

Perfect to help Yadira at the end, too.

And then, when I was already vulnerable, they revealed Fira. And why not? Ima knew about his family. *About my sister.*

There lingered a part of him that wanted to lash out… Yet why shouldn't Tano have fought so hard to protect his people? The lad *was* a good man.

Vilas exhaled. "I concede, Your Majesty. You are keener by far than even I have given you credit." And once again, a fearsome adversary.

"What I read was plain enough. You should have known as much about yourself."

"Perhaps," he replied. "I believe I can add one thing to your list."

"Please."

"Strong and principled as he is, Tano does suffer his share of doubts. I think he might not understand his true value, since he was not informed of all your choices."

"Should he have been?"

Now Vilas chuckled. "Perhaps. You wanted him wary of Lord Osidani, in case you couldn't actually trust the Fang, right? A simple reminder that Tano himself is trusted, would be enough, I'm sure."

"Very well," Ima said. "Are you now satisfied?"

"Quite nearly – I have a final request."

"Yes?"

"Let me kill your grandfather. And any surviving Luminaries."

Ima leant across the table, thumb and forefinger held close together. "You are this close to true freedom. Try again."

"I am in your debt for finding and rescuing Fira –"

"Yes, you are," Ima said, frowning now. "Think this through, Vilas. You know what is more important."

He looked to Fira, who had stopped eating now, spoon halfway to her mouth as she watched, expectant, as if waiting for shouting, violence, or an explosion of *something* unpleasant.

Time to live for something more than vengeance.

Because if he made a mistake, who would be left to teach her? She would have questions, all her life, and no-one to answer them. In her mind, rightful images of Khiya's beauty would be replaced by the Bindings in Onath. Near-extinct traditions she deserved to learn, replaced by Onath's greed.

And if the wrong person discovered her identity...

Vilas reached out to rest a hand upon hers. "All is well," he told her, the Maelohas words coming more easily now.

Chapter 34.

Vilas stared back toward Onath from where he stood on the highway's edge, stared at the Eastern Gate and the city's walls, at an entire city still very much intact.

He stared with a frown, with an urge pulling him back.

Sunlight speared through the clouds and fell on a wagon-train waiting for admittance, sounds of voices so faint they were likely imagined at such a distance. They were but a handful of thousands upon thousands of people who had no idea how close they had come to death.

"How close they could *still* be," he murmured, and the Embers called...

Vilas shook his head.

Bitterness was clearly no blossom to merely be scattered upon a breeze, it seemed.

He crossed half-trampled grass to one of the lattice-like shrines, where Fira stood examining its painted-yellow tips. Yadira watched over the girl from nearby, affixing an oat bag for her mount. "I'm a little surprised, you know," the Steel Maiden said.

"Maybe I am, too," he replied. "But this should satisfy you and the queen, right?"

"Yes. But this is not about me, is it?"

He nodded, then joined Fira. He knelt so that they were closer to eye-level. "Any *kikena* inside?"

"No." She didn't seem too disappointed, peering within, squinting at the old runes. Now, after a bath and a good night's sleep, a proper breakfast and dressed in better-fitting skirt and pants, as per Eami fashion, Fira appeared generally better. Of course, her smile did not really reach her eyes. "Maybe the next one."

"What if there isn't?" he asked.

Her smile grew. "You have to catch me one, remember?"

"I do." He sighed, exaggerating the sound somewhat. "And what if I can't? They don't often show themselves to people."

"You said you have miles and miles to try on the way to Eami."

"True enough." He glanced over at Yadira momentarily. "Fira, are you sure you want to travel all the way to Eami?"

She nodded.

"I wondered why?"

"Because Mother and Father said it was a beautiful place." She did not take her eyes from the shrine, hands tracing where the paint had run. "They said there were castles in the clouds, and that it was impossible to be sad there because everyone had such beautiful things to see."

"I have read that it is beautiful, yes," he said.

"Mmm."

"But I'm sure that people there are sad sometimes, too. Yadira would agree, if you want to ask her?"

"I know," Fira replied as her hands stopped. "You can be sad anywhere."

Now it was his turn to nod. "Will you tell me if one day you feel too sad?"

"I will."

"Good." He rose. "Let's eat something before we check the next shrine. I'm sure Yadira has something tasty for us."

"All right." She turned from the shrine but paused. "Vilas, why does your voice sound funny?"

"My voice?"

"Yes. When you say some words, it sounds… different. Not like me."

"Well… That's called an accent."

"How do you get an accent?"

"I was a prisoner in that city for a long time, so I only heard Onathians speak. And also because I'm older than you, we all spoke a little different when I was young."

"So, you're even older than you look?"

He laughed. "Yes."

A slight frown crossed her features. "I'll ask Yadira to help you, if you get tired," she said, then ran over to the Steel Maiden, and stood quietly as the woman started to pull bread and fruit from one of the saddlebags with a smile.

Vilas looked back at the city of Onath one last time. "Thank you, Fira."

Acknowledgments

Thank you to Amanda, Brooke and Shane – and to Lin and Christina :)

Ashley

A Note from Ashley

Hello! I hope you enjoyed *Knee-Deep in Cinders* and thank you for reading.

If you could help me out by leaving an honest review of the book at your place of purchase, that would be fantastic! (Long or short, bad or good, it all helps).

AND if you'd like to sign up to my newsletter (https://subscribepage.io/PLCPDM) you'll receive free eBooks, first access to preview chapters and pre-release editions of my other stories, in addition to being automatically added into the draw for giveaways.

Ashley